GRETA

GRETA

J. S. LEMON

FARRAR STRAUS GIROUX
New York

Farrar Straus Giroux Books for Young Readers
An imprint of Macmillan Publishing Group, LLC
120 Broadway, New York, NY 10271 · mackids.com

Copyright © 2024 by J. S. Lemon. All rights reserved.

Our books may be purchased in bulk for promotional, educational, or business use. Please contact your local bookseller or the Macmillan Corporate and Premium Sales Department at (800) 221-7945 ext. 5442 or by email at MacmillanSpecialMarkets@macmillan.com.

Library of Congress Cataloging-in-Publication Data
Names: Lemon, J. S., author.
Title: Greta / J.S. Lemon.
Description: First edition. | New York : Farrar Straus Giroux, 2024. | Audience: Ages 10–14. | Audience: Grades 7–9. | Summary: Seventh grader Greta grapples with feelings of inadequacy and the aftermath of sexual assault by a classmate, which leads to a transformative journey toward self-acceptance and empowerment.
Identifiers: LCCN 2023044682 | ISBN 9780374392178 (hardcover)
Subjects: CYAC: Sexual abuse–Fiction. | Metamorphosis–Fiction. | Self-acceptance–Fiction. | Middle schools–Fiction. | Schools–Fiction. | LCGFT: Novels.
Classification: LCC PZ7.1.L44475 Gr 2024 | DDC [Fic]—dc23
LC record available at https://lccn.loc.gov/2023044682

First edition, 2024
Book design by Aurora Parlagreco
Printed in the United States of America by Lakeside Book Company, Harrisonburg, Virginia

ISBN 978-0-374-39217-8

1 3 5 7 9 10 8 6 4 2

For you know who

GRETA

PROLOGUE

When I sit on the vine that grows outside my best friend Lotti's window, I have a perfect view. The leaves are wide and flat, and I can open my wings all the way, stretching their silky fabric and soaking up the last few minutes of warmth before the sun goes down. You would have to look pretty closely to be able to tell that I wasn't just another leaf. You'd have to notice that my wings are actually much more intricate, the green much bluer, closer to a pale turquoise, outlined in reddish purple. If you really looked, you would see the eyes on my wings are the shape of my father's and the hazel-green color of my mother's.

Sometimes white flowers open up on the vine that are the size of a human hand. There I can perch on a cool petal, which feels soft and powdery against the hairs on my legs. Sticking my long ribbony tongue into the center of the flower,

I can get a nice snack while I watch Lotti. It's not so different from when I used to sit in that room with her, sipping soda through a straw, listening to her talk about that doofus, Evan, who totally didn't deserve her. The juice from these flowers tastes almost the same, tingly and sweet.

There was a time when I'd be lying next to her on that purple carpet, our legs absently twined together, looking up at the blank ceiling and imagining what was going to happen when we got to eighth grade or, almost impossibly, high school.

For Lotti and everyone else I knew, that was only weeks ago.

For me, it was a lifetime.

ONE

"So which box . . . *keep*? Or *throw into a landfill where it will receive no love and ultimately contribute to the destruction of the planet*?" I held up a tiny pink plastic puppy with its tongue hanging out.

Lotti squinted her eyes and considered the little piece of plastic. "Um . . . landfill?"

"Oh my god, you're a monster, Lotti! Don't you remember how many hours we spent playing with these things?!" I walked the puppy up Lotti's pajama sleeve and made slurping noises on its behalf as it licked her face.

Lotti laughed. "How are you ever going to get through all of this stuff if you never want to throw anything away? Your mom is gonna freak."

"I don't understand," I moaned, and threw myself down

on the rug. "If we're moving to a bigger house then there's *more* space. Why do I have to get rid of anything?"

"Maybe she thinks it won't go with the decor in the *great room*," said Lotti, smiling.

"Well she's wrong," I said. "Nothing says posh like a pink plastic puppy." I grabbed the empty box labeled TRASH and threw it across the room. "This is stupid. I don't want to move. This is my house, too, how do I not even get a *vote* about this? As if I care that there's an 'open floor plan.' Isn't that just code for 'Greta will never be out of my sight'?"

"Maybe it'll be cool?" said Lotti, trying to change my mood. "Maybe you'll get your own bathroom! No more sharing with a half-potty-trained third-grade boy." She lay down next to me and gave me our signature light bonk on the nose that we've been giving each other since first grade.

I smiled and bonked her back.

"Fej doesn't want to go either," I said. My little brother, Jeff, will only write his name backward, so now (and probably forever) I call him "Fej."

Lotti realized that a change of subject was in order.

"I can't believe we're gonna be in seventh grade! Middle schoolers! That's, like, crazy," she said, staring at the ceiling.

"Oh my god." The mention of school gave me either nausea or butterflies, it was hard to tell the difference. "It's like I'm totally ready and . . . absolutely not," I said. "What if I get lost? That place is huge! I bet there are fully adult people in there who've been wandering around since they were twelve 'cause they can't find their way out! And everyone just assumes they're teachers!" A laugh rumbled up from my stomach, easy and deep, joining in perfect belly harmony with hers. In moments like these, I felt swallowed up by my love for Lotti. It was overwhelming and made my brain temporarily stop its obsession with worst-case scenarios.

"Did you hear about Sydney Coorly?" said Lotti. She was propped up on her elbow, her eyes wide. "I heard that her boobs got huge this summer, like, out of *nowhere*, bam! They just popped out!"

"Gross," I said.

"I know, but like, *some* kind of *boob situation* would be nice," said Lotti, looking down her chin at her narrow, flat chest.

"I guess." I pictured the Sydney Coorly I knew in sixth grade. Tall and long like a praying mantis, only now she had two enormous water balloons moving back and forth under her shirt like they were alive and had a mind of their own. It was horrifying.

"And Emma Torence got her period so bad that she almost bled to death. But then she recovered and now she's, like, totally . . . *wise*." Lotti squinted as she told me this deeply important information, whose source she couldn't remember.

"No way." I was intrigued. Wisdom sounded good, but maybe not at the risk of potentially life-ending blood loss.

"You think we'll get boyfriends this year?" asked Lotti with a sparkle in her eyes.

"Duh, of course. It's middle school." I paused. "I mean, I guess." I wondered what insane transformations had happened over the summer to the boys I knew. An image popped into my head of little Ryan Pollaro in his khakis and oversize sneakers, telling fart jokes through a full lumberjack beard. It was deeply disturbing.

Lotti noticed the sour look on my face and reached over and grabbed my hand. "It'll be awesome," she said. *Bonk.*

"What are you gonna wear the first day?" I looked around my room. It was covered in a multicolored layer of old toys, clothes, and books. No more organized or less cluttered than when I started this ridiculous task. I picked up a cowboy hat from a Halloween costume I wore when I was five. "Well, if I want to be irresistible, nothing says 'I'm totally grown-up' like a tiny cowboy hat!" I plopped the toddler-size hat on my head and started do-si-do-ing around the room.

Lotti rolled over laughing, and I finally collapsed onto the floor.

Something flew through the air and landed on Lotti's head. It was a crumpled-up piece of paper. She opened it.

"Oh my god," she said, laughing. There was a drawing of an evil-looking shark with a big toothy smile on its face, surrounded by pink and red hearts.

I quickly rolled over and caught my brother peeking around the door. I threw a stuffed turtle at him. "Get out, Fej!"

I heard his maniacal little laugh as he raced down the hall.

Fej absolutely loved Lotti and his need to impress her was a total pain in the butt. Every time she came over, he would bug us, trying to get her attention.

"So gross," I said, making a retching noise.

"I don't know, it's kind of sweet," she said.

I changed the subject. "My mom wants to take me back-to-school shopping," I said. "There's no way she'll let me pick what I want. She's gonna want me to get, like, a dress." I stuck out my tongue.

Lotti sat up, beaming. "We should go together! A united front! My mom could take us!"

"That would be awesome!" I said, suddenly excited. "I could tell my mom that since she has *so* much to do to get ready for the move, your mom thought it would help her out! You're brilliant!"

Lotti made *ta-da* hands.

"Wait, did you remember to bring the Book?" I asked her. She jumped up and went to her bag. The Book was the size of a dictionary and belonged to her older sister, Angie. We'd been mesmerized by it ever since we saw it sitting on Angie's bed, the sheer weight of it making it sink into her comforter. Its cover had a drawing of the sun with a human face on it, surrounded by stars and planets. It was called *The Secret Language of Your Astrological Sign*, and it absolutely held magical powers.

"Angie said if anything happened to it she would literally murder me, so don't bend the pages," said Lotti with huge, warning eyes.

I nodded as she placed it in my hands like she was entrusting me with the queen's jewels.

"Okay, do me," she said. I turned to May 20, Lotti's birthday.

"It says, 'Those born on May twentieth are highly likable people who are rarely alone. They can be eccentric, intelligent, and are usually very attractive.'"

Lotti fluttered her eyelashes.

"'When in relationships, they may have difficulty maintaining their independence and become completely absorbed by their partner.'" I gave Lotti a questioning look.

"What?" she asked, lightly punching my arm.

"I'm just saying, if you get a boyfriend this year, you better not ignore me!"

"Oh my god, Greta. That's ridiculous, we're gonna be

together forever!" She grabbed my forearm and we smiled at each other.

"My turn," I said, handing her the heavy book. I sat back and waited for her to read me my future, eager to hear explanations for my personality. I was hoping for some reassurance that I wouldn't end up living alone above some twenty-four-hour laundromat with a pet iguana.

"Okay, 'Those born on June twenty-third tend to be jovial individuals . . .'"

"Oh my god, like . . . Santa Claus?" I puffed out my cheeks and did a deep laugh while rubbing my belly.

Lotti snorted and kept reading.

"'They refuse to accept things as they are and will go to great lengths to change the circumstances of their lives.'" She looked at me under raised eyebrows. "Well, that's good, right?" she asked.

"I have no idea what that means. Just go to the relationships part."

Lotti skimmed down the page and read, "'Those born on June twenty-third tend to make wonderful companions.'"

"Great. I'm a golden retriever," I said.

I sat up on my knees and panted like a dog, threatening to lick Lotti's face.

"Stop it!" She giggled, hitting me with a pillow. She kept reading.

"'They are the social butterflies of the astrology world. They tend to get restless and bored but can often provide creative ideas to solve complex problems.'"

"This is stupid," I said, yawning. We lay next to each other in my bed, surrounded by an ocean of stuff. Stuff that my mom wanted me to throw away.

TWO

When we came down to breakfast the next morning, we had to dodge a bunch of boxes marked KITCHEN. My dad was scrolling through his phone, his jaws working hard to try to chew the turkey bacon that my mom insists he eat. She saw his exaggerated effort and sighed.

"It's good for you, Paul. And it tastes exactly the same."

"The same as what? A tongue depressor?" muttered my dad. The bacon made a *clink* sound on the plate when he dropped it to gulp down an entire glass of water.

He winked at me. "Morning, sunshine," he said. "How are you, Lotti? Did you get any sleep?"

"Yup, slept like a log, Mr. Goodwin," said Lotti. It was like a script; every time she slept over they said the exact same thing at breakfast.

"Good morning, you two," said my mom with a smile that was definitely because Lotti was there.

"Morning, Mrs. G.," answered Lotti.

"My eyes feel weird," I said, rubbing them.

"What's your plan today, girls?" Mom asked, ignoring my comment. "Did you make a dent in that mess of a room?" She was fiercely focused on tying her running shoes. My mom is constantly working on maintaining her appearance, like she's a sculpture made out of sand and the tide is coming in.

Lotti and I were pouring spoonfuls of sugar on our cereal so it wouldn't taste like shredded cardboard. Which, I'm sure, is exactly what it was.

"Oh yeah, I'm throwing tons of stuff away." Lotti and I snuck in a secret smile.

"Good. Well there's a lot to do around here before we move, and school starts in less than a week."

As if we didn't know that.

She looked like she was praying to the fitness gods as she stretched against the counter. "It's a beautiful day. Get outdoors, move your bodies."

I just had to wait these things out. My mom usually seemed deeply concerned with how I spent my time for about two minutes, then she was off "improving herself." She was probably headed to the gym to go to her twerking class, and just the thought of her shaking her butt around with a bunch of other moms thinking they look sexy almost made me gag on my multigrain oat flakes.

Fej stumbled into the kitchen in his Iron Man jammies. Because Lotti was there, he immediately went into entertainment mode. He started drumming on all the boxes, eventually flopping into a chair.

"Fej, stop! You're being such a pain!" I whined.

He stuck his tongue out at me and smiled at Lotti.

"I'm really good at drumming," he said with a shrug.

"I can see that," she said.

"I'll probably have my own band one day. We'll be called Fart Attack," he said, launching into a symphony of disgusting noises.

"Eww!" Lotti said, laughing.

"Oh my god! You're so gross! Mom! Make him stop!"

My mom was still stretching and she looked like she wanted a teacher to call on her as she pulled one arm above her head, yanking at it with the other hand. "Jeffrey, that's enough. Remember, you have a baseball game at eleven thirty. Dad's taking you. Paul, don't forget to bring a snack."

"How about I bring this turkey bacon. They can use it as a bat, it's basically made of wood." He swung the bacon like a miniature baseball bat and made a clicking noise with his tongue.

Fej laughed and shouted, "Home run!" while pumping his fists in the air. Then he went back to shoveling cereal into his mouth. He turned and looked at me closely for the first time since he had come downstairs.

"What's wrong with you?" he said, milk dribbling down his chin.

"What are you talking about?" I said, rubbing my eyes with the backs of my hands.

"You look like a fly when you do that," he said. He mimicked my movements while sticking out his tongue and darting his eyes around the room.

"Shut up, I do not." I said. "Mom, can I sleep over at Lotti's tomorrow night?"

Mom gave her usual response: "Is it okay with her mother?"

"Yeah she's fine with it, Mrs. G.," said Lotti in her talking-to-parents voice. Her family was so big that one more person in the house was never an issue. I basically had an open invitation.

I started counting the hours until I could get away from all these boxes.

THREE

"I'm definitely not coming out," I said from behind the flimsy changing room curtain.

"C'mon, let me see." Lotti pulled a small part of the curtain back so all I saw was her big brown eyes and shiny metal smile.

"Lotti, I look ridiculous! They make me look like I've got mom-butt!" I turned around to give her the full effect. "Like, it starts halfway up my back!" I clenched my butt cheeks and did my best imitation of my mom: "'You girls should really wear clothes that fit you and flatter your figure.'"

She snorted a laugh and swatted at me weakly.

Lotti's mom came into the dressing room carrying a pink shirt with daisies all over it. It was something that Lotti would never wear and she rolled her eyes.

"Mom, that is hideous."

"Just try it on, it'll look so cute on you!" She handed it to her and looked at me over Lotti's shoulder.

"Oh Greta! You're so lovely and lanky! Like a daddy longlegs!"

I smiled at her. "Thanks, Mrs. Messina," I said.

Lotti laughed. "You look amazing, Greta. The jeans are just weird. Try on that blue shirt."

I gave her a dramatic sigh and closed the curtain.

When I came back out, Lotti was wearing a green version of the same shirt. Only the straps that were showing under her shirt were shiny and black and very different from the ones on my bra, which was basically a glorified tank top with a layer of *support* that I didn't really need.

My voice was just on the edge between a whisper and a scream. "Are you wearing an actual *bra*?" I suddenly felt like I did when I was six years old and Lotti was showing me the new iPad she'd gotten from her grandmother.

"Yeah, my mom said I could get one." Lotti seemed taller, older.

My mouth was hanging open. "Lotti, you look *hot*, like, *high school* hot. I'm so jealous!"

"Maybe you could get one, too?" she said, shrugging. She knew that the chances of my mother agreeing to let me get a real bra, not to mention one that was *black*, were zero. I might as well ask her if I could get a neck tattoo.

"Yeah, right," I said, rolling my eyes. I pulled the curtain closed with a dramatic *swish*.

"Let's see if we can pick up some pizza for dinner on the way home!" said Lotti from behind her curtain. Was it my imagination or did even her voice sound more mature now?

"Totally," I said.

While Lotti and her mom argued about where to go to get the pizza, I stood in front of the full-length mirror before putting my clothes back on. My fake tank-top bra glowed under the store's lights like a bright flag, reminding me: *Not yet, not yet . . .*

When we got back to Lotti's we brought our dinner up to her room so we could have some privacy and look at our loot from the day.

"I really think Evan S. is gonna notice me this year," said Lotti, holding up her new jeans.

"If he doesn't, then he's an idiot," I said. But I wasn't really paying attention. The moon was coming in through the window, giving everything a slightly bluish glow.

"He's so cute and funny," she said dreamily.

"If you say so," I answered. The light was making the curtains bloom into a pearly gray color.

"Let's go outside!" I said.

"It's, like, nine o'clock, and we're in our pajamas," said Lotti, looking at me like I'd suggested white water rafting.

"It's amazing out there!" I said. My body felt drawn to the front yard. I had a sudden urge to lie spread-eagle in the silver-coated grass.

I started toward the door.

"Wait! Let me get my slippers on at least. And be *quiet*!" We hurried down the stairs.

As soon as we opened the front door it was like we were stepping onto the moon itself. My pajamas were white with owls on them. In the moonlight they were glowing as if they were lit by a neon sign.

The whole yard, the whole neighborhood, was transformed. Everything had turned a muted version of its usual color. Like a blue filter was shining on the world, making it peaceful and strange.

I started skipping and twirling around Lotti. "Isn't it amazing?!" I sang.

"Shhhh!" Lotti couldn't help but giggle while she scolded me. "You're certifiable," she said.

The moon was huge, but not quite full, so it looked more like an oval, like a face.

"Okay, let's go back in before my mom comes out and yells at us," whispered Lotti.

I looked down at my hands; my skin was a powdery blue. I felt beautiful.

Lotti started tugging on my sleeve and I let her pull me toward the front door while I stared at the face of the moon. I felt like I was basking in something like love, like the moon was doing this, lighting up the world, just for me. I stumbled backward toward the house.

FOUR

I woke up Monday morning already nervous about school, even though it was still twenty-four hours away. I'd wanted to spend the day with Lotti going over every scenario that might come up, making sure we were absolutely prepared for the mayhem that was *definitely* waiting for us.

But my mom had other plans.

She had taken the day off work so that we could go to the school together to get my ID and walk through the building. This way I'd know where I needed to go tomorrow.

When we were getting into the car, Fej jumped into the back seat.

"What are you doing? You're not coming with us!" My voice was on the verge of a scream. The idea of my little brother running around the middle school making fart noises while I tried to look like I belonged there was unfathomable.

"Of course he's coming, Greta. I can't leave him at home alone. And you'll behave yourself, won't you, Jeffrey?" She smiled at him in the rearview mirror. He gave her an innocent nod. But as soon as she turned back around, he looked at me with a huge demonic grin. He was rubbing his hands together like a criminal mastermind.

"Oh my god," I said, sinking into my seat. "This can*not* be happening."

The parking lot was full when we got to the school. Some of the parents just sat in their cars, scrolling through their phones while they waited for their kids. But not my mom. We were going in *as a family*. She took off her seat belt, and I made a hysterical plea, holding on to her arm with both my hands.

"Please, Mom, please, please, please can I just go in by myself?" I begged her.

She was shaking her head no. So I pulled out the only argument that had even the *slightest* chance of working.

"Mom, I know you want to help me, but I have to learn to do this myself. I'm in middle school now. I'm thirteen. This is really important." I tried to make my voice as calm and grown-up as possible.

There were a few seconds of silence while my mom looked at me like I was asking her if I could buy a motorcycle. But then something passed over her face. She took a deep breath and touched my shoulder.

"Okay. Fine, sweetie. Jeffrey and I will be over there." She pointed to the baseball field next to the school.

I kissed her on the cheek and ran out of the car.

I felt like I was walking into an airport. I hadn't been in a building this big since we flew to Baltimore to see my grandparents. There were signs everywhere, saying things like COMMITMENT!

CONFIDENCE!

CHARACTER!

It seemed like a lot of pressure to put on us as soon as we walked in the door. A woman wearing a lanyard that said STAFF introduced herself as Mrs. Redmond and pointed to a room marked STUDENT IDS.

I stood in line, trying to look like this was all so utterly boring, and I was absolutely *not* having a panic attack.

"Next," said a man in khakis that were straining at the seams. It was nine o'clock in the morning and he already had circles of sweat darkening his maroon shirt. He looked sleepy with boredom as he motioned toward a stool in front of a pale blue screen. I sat down and tried to quickly come up with the exact kind of smile I wanted to represent me. I was trying to put on a smile that said *I'm Greta, and I'm totally cool with absolutely anything that comes my way*, when I heard, "Next," in the same bored voice.

I froze and looked at the sweaty man who was now directing a short, freckly boy with a freshly shaved mohawk to my stool.

He already took the *picture*?! I thought about the faces I must've been making while I was concentrating and I suddenly felt nauseous.

As I left the little room, a woman with a huge smile handed me a small tote bag. "Welcome to Maple Ave. Middle School!" she said.

I walked as fast as I could back through the glass doors toward my mom's car. I just wanted to go home.

FIVE

Stepping into the school building the next day was like walking into the middle of a six-lane highway. How was it possible that everyone else seemed to know exactly where they were going?

There were kids I recognized from elementary school, who looked pretty much the same. But then there were kids who looked like college students. Some of them were about six feet tall with shoulders that stretched their T-shirts across muscly backs. There were girls wearing gobs and gobs of makeup that made it impossible to tell if they were even nervous. Their eyes had turned black and spidery, impenetrable. The only thing my face was covered in was fear.

Lotti and I, wearing *almost* matching T-shirts that we had spent the night before carefully picking out, gave each other an encouraging look. By some stroke of pure luck, we were in the same homeroom, and as we stepped into the traffic, I felt Lotti's forearm brush against mine. Without that I don't know if I could've moved an inch.

I'm not sure if I breathed during the entire fifteen minutes of homeroom before the bell rang for first period. But I didn't pass out, so that seemed like a good sign. Lotti gave me one last panicked look as we were swept up in separate currents down the hallways. I wouldn't see her again until lunch.

My first class was science. I settled into the back row and immediately noticed that the room felt serious. There weren't cartoony pictures all over the walls of rain clouds and big purple flowers. No basketball-size Styrofoam planets hanging from the ceiling, like in Mrs. Welchman's class last year.

The science teacher, Mr. Lee, told us to settle down and welcomed us to seventh-grade life science.

"Hey everybody, I'm Mr. Lee and this year we're going to learn a lot about *life*!"

When he said this, he looked like a preacher in a movie, throwing his hands in the air dramatically.

He looked around the room at the half-asleep kids and dialed back his enthusiasm.

"One of the questions we'll be answering is, How do we know if something is alive? Any ideas?" He paused, waiting for hands to shoot up in the air with potential answers.

Someone coughed.

"Okay, well, it seems like an easy question, but it's not, is it?" He started going through a list of things that had to be true for something to be considered alive.

"First of all, it has to be made up of cells, the smallest units of life."

He showed us a boring picture of shapes that looked like the inside of droopy avocados and started to write down a bunch of words like *nucleus* and *vacuole* as he pointed to the blobs inside of them. I'd heard the word *nucleus* before, but *vacuole* sounded like something he shouldn't be saying out loud. He saw that he was losing us. "We'll be looking at a variety of different cells this year. I'll have you scrape some cells from your cheek, and we can look at them up close under the microscope." My tongue went immediately to the inside of my cheek. *Scrape* sounded painful.

"Also, for something to be considered alive, it has to show movement." Now he was showing us a video. We watched as a bug wandered casually on a leaf, oblivious (in my mind it was whistling), when suddenly the leaf turned into a creature with sharp teeth and swallowed it whole. Mr. Lee smiled when some of the girls let out an "aww . . ." like that bug was a cute little bunny rabbit and this was the saddest thing they'd ever seen.

Seriously? I thought. *You didn't see that coming? You've never heard of a Venus flytrap?* Mr. Lee kept going.

"In order for something to be classified as *alive*, it has to respond to a stimulus; a stimulus is an activity that causes a response. Can anyone tell me what an example of a stimulus might be?"

"Setting something on fire?" said Dylan Taylor. It was a typical response from Dylan, who would probably spend time in jail as an adult.

"Well, sure," said Mr. Lee, appearing to make a mental note to keep an eye on Dylan. "An organism can detect a stimulus in many ways, through sight, touch, smell, sound. Anything that changes its environment."

Well, I thought, *that's one way to put how I've felt since starting middle school: alive.*

"And of course, everyone's favorite, the ability to reproduce."

There were some muffled laughs and obnoxious fake coughs popping up around the room.

"Yes, it's very exciting." Mr. Lee rolled his eyes, he probably had seen this reaction from middle schoolers every single year of his career as a teacher. He went on, unfazed. "We'll be talking about reproduction this year. Both sexual and asexual. Can anyone tell me the difference?"

More laughter.

"Maybe this video will help."

I could feel the whole room hold its breath . . . Oh my god, he's not gonna show us . . . ? The video he showed was *not* what the coughers and laughers in the room were hoping for. It was just a blue background with these things that looked like fuzzy Tic Tacs moving jerkily around in a little group. "These are cells that are reproducing. Each individual cell can reproduce by itself, which is called *asexual* reproduction. We'll discuss sexual reproduction later." There were some groans of disappointment, but I think most of us were a bit relieved.

"Another characteristic of something that is alive is *growth and development*." There was some snickering. Sydney Coorly was sitting in front of me, perfectly still. Even though all I could see was the back of her head, I remembered what Lotti had told me. I was sure that she could read the room and wanted this man to move on to the next topic . . . quickly.

"Growth and change are vital to all living things." I felt the strap of my empty bra slip limply down my shoulder.

So much for being considered "alive," I thought, sinking closer to the top of my desk.

Standing in the doorway of the cafeteria, searching frantically for Lotti, I was sure that I would spontaneously combust. It was chaos. Hundreds of kids talking at once in a giant windowless room with nowhere for the sound to go. Laughter, squealing, and just plain talking filled the air, but the thing that made it so thick, made the air feel like something that would make me choke, was the desperation that was radiating off everyone with a stinky heat. Eyes darting around, searching for the perfect place to sit. The impossible task of trying not to look pathetic as you carried your red plastic tray like an offering of your soul from table to table. *These mushy foods represent my personality. Would you mind if I placed them next to your soggy tater tots?* This was it. First day of school. Chances were whoever you ended up sitting with was someone you'd be stuck with for a year.

Suddenly I got a glimpse of long dark hair. "Lotti!" I yelled. This, of course, went against my usual strategy of *above all, do not call attention to yourself*, but I didn't care. I rushed over to her, and we hugged like soldiers coming back from war.

"Oh my god, this is crazy! Did you get lost? There's so much work! These teachers are delusional if they think we can do all of this!" We stood in line for our lukewarm pizza with a side of wilty salad.

"At least they have a five star restaurant," said Lotti, making a face.

The cafeteria lady glared.

When we were safely at a table it felt like we could breathe for the first time in hours.

"Evan S. is in my algebra class," Lotti said in a totally

normal voice. But her eyes were the size of the pepperoni on her droopy pizza.

"Okay . . ." I waited for more information.

Her big metal smile sparkled in the fluorescent cafeteria lights. "He was sitting across the aisle from me, and we looked at each other and rolled our eyes at the same time when Ms. Pyott started talking about how this year was going to be so tough and how we better do our homework blah blah blah."

"Lotti! Oh my god!" Seeing her eyes light up made me feel happy and lonely at the same time. "I'm so happy for you!" I gushed.

Just then Sydney Coorly walked by our table. I stared directly at her chest, I couldn't help myself. She was wearing a T-shirt that said I CLIMBED MT. WASHINGTON. Only the word WASHINGTON was slightly distorted as it stretched across her new breasts.

Had she worn a T-shirt that talked about *mountains* on purpose? I was so jealous and about to say something to Lotti when I noticed another way that Sydney looked different. She was always the tallest girl in the class, but somehow it looked like she'd gotten shorter. Her shoulders pointed in front of her slightly, like little folded wings, trying to protect her chest. She had a big smile on her face as her eyes darted nervously around the room. I wondered if I was the only one who saw the look of terror in her face, like a gazelle being stalked by lions in one of those nature shows.

It seemed like the whole cafeteria got slightly quieter as she walked by. Except for the *Hey Sydney*s that didn't all seem friendly.

When Sydney had passed by, I felt a dull ache of sadness. But I'm not sure if it was for her or for me.

"Oh my god, they're ginormous," whispered Lotti.

SIX

When I got home from school on Wednesday, my mom started nagging me again about getting rid of stuff. It seemed like she couldn't wait to get out of this house, like everything in it was old and ugly. But I loved our house. I loved the weird musty smell of the basement as I would rush down the stairs to get whatever my mom had sent me down there for (before "whatever was down there" got me).

I loved the secret spot under my bed where I had written on the floor in kindergarten. I remember how hard it was to see under there while I carefully spelled out the words MOM IS DUM. Above them was a drawing of her angry face with horns. She had yelled at me and put me in a time-out for drawing on the kitchen table, so it seemed like a perfectly reasonable response. So far, she hadn't seen this particular masterpiece.

I loved the sound of the refrigerator door: *Wheh . . . wheh* like there was someone in there playing a tiny out-of-tune horn. It made sneaking food nearly impossible, but the sound of it always made me smile. I loved hearing the canned laugh track of a sitcom through my bedroom floor as my parents watched TV. My dad would mumble something, and my mom would laugh in a way that I never heard when Fej and I were in the room. I would picture them sitting next to each other on the couch, like regular people, before they were parents.

And my room was my island. I was the mayor, the president, and the queen. Like me, it pretty much looked the same as when I was little but with more chaos. Old toys and dolls were still scattered around the room. Only they were almost transformed now, merging with a sea of clothes and other junk. The walls, still painted a peachy-pink color, had been covered in posters of my favorite bands, random stickers, and Christmas lights.

I sat in front of the mirror and scrolled through my phone. There were tons of pictures of me and Lotti over the past couple of years. If you wanted to put them in chronological order, you'd have to mostly refer to the clothes. Or Lotti's hair. Her mom made her get the same haircut, a short bob with straight bangs, until fourth grade. It basically looked like LEGO hair, like a black helmet that she could take off before bed every night. But now it was long and shiny, hanging halfway down her back in loose, curving waves. It was beautiful.

I, however, looked exactly the same as I did in elementary

school. It wasn't a terrible face; everything was basically in the right place. But there it was, staring back at me. Evidence that it had basically not changed since first grade. Except I had slightly worse skin. My cheeks were still chubby and covered with a handful of freckles that only brought more attention to them. My thick curly hair was the color of wet sand and had been wrestled into a ponytail in every single picture. Somehow I had dodged the whole "palate expander, braces" nightmare, which Lotti kept reminding me I was so lucky for. But even that seemed to be proof that nothing was changing. Not even my teeth.

I'd gotten comments like *Greta, you have such amazing curls!* as long as I could remember. But no one was trying to make *their* hair frizzy with wispy little hairs like cobwebs flying around their foreheads. It was all about long, straight, and shiny, so I never really took it as a compliment. I was in middle school now. Something had to give.

Weaving around boxes piled throughout the living room like an obstacle course, I made my way to my mom, who was hunched over her laptop.

"Mom, can I *please, please, please* get a haircut?! I look like a baby."

My hair has always been a huge issue between me and my mom. For some reason it seems to be the one thing she will not let go of. I think, to her, it's a reminder that I will "always be her little girl." It's like that story about the guy who loses all his power when a woman cuts off his hair. Except that woman is my mom, and she's the one who would lose her power. It's creepy.

"But Greta, your hair is so pretty," she said, holding my ponytail in her open palm like it was a piece of priceless jewelry that I couldn't possibly appreciate. "Besides, when you can pull your hair back you can see those big, beautiful eyes of yours!"

"I'm so sick of it, *please*!!!" I grabbed at the ends of my hair and pulled them like a wet towel that was weighing my whole body down. I was desperate. I dropped to my knees. I was determined to continue this dramatic scene until she finally gave in this time.

"Well, you'd have to take care of it, Greta. Shorter hair takes more work. Your hair is pretty thick and curly. A haircut will mean you have to spend a little more time with it in the morning . . ." This *work* that my mom was referring to was a full-time job for her. She spent tons of time in the bathroom primping and perfecting. Everything had to be just right. I knew she felt this was the duty of every woman, to look as beautiful as possible. And it seemed exhausting. Because I'm her daughter, my appearance seems to fall under the category of her appearance. Why else would she care what I did with my hair? It had nothing to do with her.

But now didn't seem to be the time to have that particular

argument. We were close to a breakthrough, I could feel it. So I closed my eyes, letting her know that I was fully aware of this great responsibility and completely up for the task as I nodded like a bobblehead.

She rolled her eyes and did a dramatic sigh. After what seemed like five minutes, she finally said, "Fine. But not too short."

I threw my arms around her and ran back up to my room to call Lotti.

"Whoa! I can't believe it, she finally said yes?" said Lotti.

We spent the next hour sending each other pictures of glamorous women. Their loose curls hung weightlessly on their shoulders, pieces of hair falling perfectly in front of one eye. Because apparently if you're that sexy, you only need to see out of one eye.

Mom drummed her nails on my door.

"Okay, you're all set. I made you an appointment with Kaitlyn at Tress Transformations for Thursday after school."

I squealed into the phone. I just knew that this haircut was gonna change my life. I pictured myself walking down the halls in school in slow motion, a sweep of sexy bangs in my eyes. Everyone would stop in mid-conversation to turn, open-mouthed, and say something to their friends like, *I never knew Greta Goodwin was so incredibly beautiful! She doesn't even need to see out of both of her eyes, so mysterious!*

It was gonna be great.

SEVEN

When I got home from the salon on Thursday, I immediately called Lotti.

"Well?!" She answered the phone on the first ring. "Do you love it? Do you look older?"

"If by older you mean do I look like a middle-aged woman who crochets outfits for her cats? Then yes."

"Let me see it. FaceTime me right now," she demanded.

When I saw Lotti's face on the screen I started crying again. I had been crying since I left the salon and my head hurt. The whole ride home, my mom kept telling me how cute I looked and reaching over to touch my hair that had been covered in a thick coat of sticky hairspray until it felt like I was wearing a wig. That would have literally been better. Then I could take it off and shove it down the garbage disposal.

"Cute?! That's like, the exact opposite of what I want to be, Mom!"

She rubbed my arm as she drove. "Well, I think you look great," she said.

Somehow, that made me feel even worse.

Lotti looked at me, my thick, frizzy bangs like a giant old-timey mustache stuck to my forehead. My curls, since they were no longer weighted down, had suddenly been given the freedom to poof out to their heart's content. My head looked like a triangle.

She took one look at me and said, with a completely dead-serious face, "You look so hot!"

"I do *not*," I whined.

"I'm coming over right now," she said as she hung up. I buried my face in my pillow.

Lotti's house was only down the block, and she must've run the whole way. I don't know how she was able to do it, but when I opened the door and she saw my ridiculous hair in person, she still did not laugh.

We went right up to my room.

"I can totally work with this," she said, sitting me down on the bed. She got out her bag full of supplies and went to work.

"We just have to get this stuff out of it," she said. She dunked my head in the bathroom sink. I felt the warm water rushing over my eyes as I squeezed them tightly shut. Lotti's fingers were rubbing shampoo into my scalp, and it gave me a glimmer of hope. If anyone could make this better, it was her.

After putting on some styling crème that smelled like coconuts, she got out a special brush that she'd brought with her and started blow-drying my curls into some sort of submission. It was like trying to teach a feral cat to walk on a leash. Each time she pulled out a curl it stubbornly sprang back into place. But she had the patience of a saint, and I watched as my frizz deflated, just a bit. Next, she put some sort of gel in her palms and smoothed her hands over my limp curls. When she was through, we both looked at me in the mirror. It wasn't great. I did *not* look like any of the women in those pictures, but it was better. Lotti smiled at me over my head and unlike the woman in the salon who seemed to only look at herself when she talked to me, she was looking right at me when she said, "You're beautiful, Greta."

EIGHT

Ms. Binney, in a beige-on-beige ensemble that made her almost disappear, was talking about *Lord of the Flies* in third-period English. But considering how packed that story is with *boy* nonsense, without a girl in sight, it was hard to pay attention. Even if they were trying to kill each other.

I thought about what this book would be like if it was a bunch of girls trapped on an island. First of all, I'm sure it would be much less disgusting. There would definitely be fighting, but it would be different, much less obvious. I can see Piggy (would they call her Ms. Piggy?) getting the brunt of all the bullying, but she wouldn't know it at first. *Why do I hate myself so much?* she would wonder. Not noticing that the popular girls had been eating away at her self-esteem for months as they sunned on the beach in little bikinis they'd made out of leaves.

I felt a searing heat coming from a few desks over. It was like someone was shining a laser beam at my face. When I got up the courage to sneak a look at where it was coming from, I saw Derek Thompson . . . staring at me. I knew him from sixth grade but had barely spoken to him. He had dirty-blond hair, and his gums were too big for his mouth, but he had a swagger. He had somehow escaped the constant self-doubt that plagued most of us, and that was almost like a superpower. He was draped over his desk, resting his head in his hand, facing directly at me. He was making no attempt to hide his stare. I tried to play it cool and pretend I didn't even notice this virtual spotlight on the side of my face.

My life strategy, as I've mentioned, is *Above all, do not call attention to yourself*, but this was different. It was like Derek's eyes had plugged into me, and my whole body was shooting off sparks. I could tell, without looking at him, where exactly *he* was looking at *me*. I was suddenly aware of the outrageous number of clips in my hair, what earrings I had worn, what position my shoulder was in. I arranged my pose like he was an artist painting me, trying to find the most elegant and sophisticated way to sit in a small metal desk. At first, I thought he might make some obnoxious comment about all my barrettes. But he didn't say a word.

Suddenly there was a loud sound like a dying cow. Ms. Binney was blowing into a pinkish and slightly yellow conch shell the size of a rotisserie chicken that she had brought into class to "keep learning fresh and exciting!"

She beamed. "This conch shell is just like the one Ralph uses on the island to get everyone's attention!" Her excitement over the shell seemed like a mistake when talking about warfare among children.

Everyone was laughing except Derek. He was still staring at me.

The bell rang and a few kids went up to Ms. Binney's desk trying to get a turn blowing into the shell.

I tried to slither out of my seat in a fluid movement that said *Everything I do is effortless and fascinating, and I totally don't notice you at all.* I banged my knee on the metal bar under my desk but harnessed the power of Zeus not to let it show. Then everyone was standing up and getting their stuff together, forming a barrier between us. I moved toward the door as fast as I could without running, desperate to find Lotti.

I found her at her locker. I clung to her arm like it was a life preserver as I quickly told her about Derek, the adrenaline pumping through my body.

"Oh my god Greta, that is so creepy!" she said. But on her wide-eyed face there was the beginning of a smile. "He's totally into you!" Someone rammed me in the shoulder with their backpack, which I hardly noticed.

"It was crazy!" I thought about the look in Derek's eyes as he aimed them relentlessly at my face. I felt different. Like

Derek's attention had changed me somehow. I had become something worth looking at . . . almost pretty. *This is what is supposed to happen in middle school*, I thought. You get a boyfriend or a girlfriend. I might have been getting ahead of myself, but something was definitely going on. His attention made me feel included. Like I wasn't an impostor, some little kid sneaking around the middle school hoping no one would notice.

Lotti's eyes were sparkling as she asked me if I liked him.

"I don't know, he's kinda cute. I never thought about him before," I said. My head felt like it was about to spin off my neck and bounce around the hallway like a drone in the hands of a mad scientist.

"Well he obviously likes you," she said. She reached over and bonked my nose. We had exactly three minutes until we had to be at our next class, so we had to be quick.

A teacher walked through the swarm of the hallway and warned, "Let's go, people! No dillydallying!"

"I want to know *everything*," said Lotti, closing her locker. I nodded as I thought, *I think I've already told you everything*.

He looked at me.

I almost died.

End of story.

We set off for our next classes, our fingers stretching toward each other as long as possible.

At dinner, Fej was going on endlessly about how he had so much homework in third grade and didn't have time for baseball and how school was stupid and why did he have to learn about language arts when he already knew how to speak and why did he need to know where Bolivia was when he was never gonna go there . . .

My parents sat, mesmerized.

Finally they turned their attention toward me.

"How about you, Greta?" asked my mom.

"I don't know. It's fine." I shrugged. "We have to read *Lord of the Flies*, which is stupid."

"A book about flies? I bet *you* like that, Greta, since you look like one!" Fej started doing his fly imitation again, his eyes darting around the room as he licked the backs of his hands and rubbed them together.

I reached over to pinch him in the arm but got a warning look from my dad.

I did have a headache and rubbed at my eyes (in a completely normal, human way!).

"Are you okay, honey?" my mom asked me. "Are your eyes bothering you? Maybe you need glasses?"

Great, I thought. The final touch to go with my flat chest and old-lady haircut, *glasses*. I'd rather be blind.

"Oh, and this came in the mail today!" She got up from the table and tried not to smile as she handed me my school ID.

It was worse than I thought. I had a look on my face like I

had just noticed that the photographer was wearing a gorilla suit. My expression was an *ever so attractive* combination of confusion and horror. My hair was pulled back in a ponytail so tight that all you could see of it was a halo of frizz around my huge pasty forehead. Fej jumped up from his chair and snuck behind me to see it.

"Greta! What is *wrong* with you?!" He bent over laughing hysterically, and I swatted in his direction.

"Perfect," I said, shoving the ID into my back pocket. I pushed back from the table, my water glass teetering dangerously as I did, and stomped out of the room.

The whole way up the stairs, I felt like I was going to cry. My eyes were throbbing like they were gonna pop out of my head. Great. So my boobs aren't getting any bigger, but my *eyes* are growing? They're already huge! People have been telling me I have big, beautiful eyes since I was little. Ugh.

A few minutes later Mom tapped her fingernails on my door. That drove me crazy. Why couldn't she just knock like everyone else?

"What?" I said, my voice muffled in my pillow. She pushed the door open just enough to see the wreckage that was my room.

"Greta! We're leaving in six weeks! You haven't packed a thing! This place is a pigsty!" She started picking up random things and throwing them into the box labeled TRASH.

"Mom! I'll do it! Stop!" I sprang out of bed and grabbed the box.

"Six weeks, Greta. You have six weeks." She looked at me from under her perfectly shaped eyebrows.

"This is stupid, I don't even want to go," I snarled.

My mom moved a pile of stuff on my bed so she'd have somewhere to sit and patted the space next to her. I plopped down, refusing to look at her.

"You're gonna love the new house, Greta. It's beautiful! There's so much more room and the light is fantastic. It's not like we're moving to another town, it's just fifteen minutes from here. We'll go see it together tomorrow, after school, you're going to fall in love with it!" She laid her hand on my knee. "Your room is bigger than this one and you and Jeffrey will have your own bathroom!" She said this like it was a good thing, smiling at me as if I was a toddler. I pictured myself sitting on a single bed in the middle of some beige, empty room, waiting for my brother to get out of the bathroom so I could shut myself in there and cry.

"You'll still be able to see Lotti all the time." She put her arm around me. I wouldn't look at her. I'd heard all of this stuff before. "Space and light" seemed like lame reasons to leave everything you know and love. And fifteen minutes was far enough that Lotti and I wouldn't be able to walk to each other's houses, so it might as well have been Cleveland.

After a bit of silence, Mom took a deep breath. "I know

you don't want to leave, Greta. But I've been in this house for a long time, years before you were even born, and I really need a change. Your dad and I have been saving and planning for a place like this since you were little. It's a big deal that we can finally move to our dream home. I promise you, once you get used to it, it'll be like you've always lived there."

I gave her a look that showed I did *not* believe that this would be true.

"You'll see tomorrow. It's not the actual house, ours is still being built, but we'll go to one that's just like it, and then you can see how beautiful it's going to be!" I rolled my eyes but she kept going.

"I know change is hard, sweetie." We looked at each other in silence. She reached up and wound her pinkie around mine. We had done this as long as I could remember. It was a secret signal, just between the two of us. It meant a lot of things, I guess. But mostly it meant . . . *I'm here. I love you. Everything is going to be okay.* No matter what was going on, this gesture could make me feel better about something without saying a single word. Even now, when I was determined to sit perfectly still in defiance, I could feel the fist of my body loosen just a little.

"Well," she said, patting my leg and standing up. "You'll see. In the meantime, think of this as a new stage of maturity. You can start fresh, everything will be brand-new! And I don't think that *this thing* has a place in the next chapter of your life." She held up a plastic brontosaurus that I used to chew on as a toddler. There were teeth marks all over its neck like it had been mauled by a T. rex.

"If you think I'm leaving Wonto behind, you're sadly mistaken," I said.

She smiled and closed the door behind her.

NINE

"Oh good! You found it!" sang the real estate agent. She looked like she was wearing a helmet made out of yellow straw with enough hair spray in it to make a hole in the ozone layer directly above her head. She had layers of makeup on her face that ended right at her jawline, as if someone had stuck her painted head on someone else's body.

The neighborhood was an endless maze of identical houses in different stages of being finished. We'd actually driven around in circles three times before my mom finally recognized the Realtor's car in the driveway.

The four of us walked up a sidewalk that was lined in pink and white flowers that must've just been planted. They were spaced perfectly apart like a reluctant little welcoming committee, still droopy and looking about as happy to be there as I was. A sign as big as Fej leaned next to the front door. It had

WELCOME written on it in huge, vertical letters. It felt as if we were being lured into a trap. This house was trying way too hard to get us to come in. My stomach knotted.

With a smile that looked like it might crack her face open, the real estate lady introduced herself to me and my brother as Kelly Kelliher.

Kelly Kelliher? Are you kidding me? For a split second I got a wave of hope: *Maybe this whole thing is a joke?*

"Hi," I said, forcing a smile.

Fej looked like he might explode. His little body was tense with the desire to pick up everything he saw.

There was a scented candle burning in the kitchen that was supposed to convince us that she had just baked cookies, and I felt a headache coming on.

"I've met your parents already. I've heard so much about you!"

Well, Kelly Kelliher, I seriously doubt any of it is true, I thought. But I smiled.

As we walked around the house it seemed like we were on a movie set. There were fake apples in a shiny purple bowl and plants with vinyl leaves sitting in pots full of plastic dirt. Too many pillows lined each piece of beige furniture, reminding us not to even *think* about sitting down. There were some paintings on the walls that must have been done by a computer that was set on "abstract ocean": blobs of blue and gray.

My mom might as well have been at Disney World. Her

eyes were shimmering as she ran her fingers along a countertop that was sparkling with flecks of gold.

"Of course, the granite look would be an upgrade," said Kelly Kelliher, not wanting my mom to get the wrong idea about what she was *really* getting in her version of this place.

Fej, meanwhile was running around the house picking up every ugly knickknack he saw, the gold horse head that was supposed to look old but still had the gooey traces of a price sticker on its neck, the block of wood that was imitating a shelf of books, some metal-and-glass oval thing that was trying to be sculpture. I thought Kelly Kelliher might have a stroke.

"Please don't touch that, sweetie, it's not a toy," she said through a forced smile.

Isn't it, though, Kelly? I thought. *Aren't we all just pretending this is a real house?*

My dad was looking at windowsills and cabinets, probably looking for *shoddy craftsmanship* as he answered my mom's constant rhetorical question "Isn't this great, Paul?" with "It's great, Maggie, really great." He didn't seem any more fooled by this place that was pretending to be a house than we did.

My dad's the kind of person who could live under a bridge as long as he was allowed to bring his corduroy recliner. He's a man of few needs. My mom got him a sweater one Christmas and he literally said, "It's great, honey! But I already have a sweater."

The truth was, though, that he was madly in love with my mom and if this spooky fake house made her happy, it was all right with him.

"You kids will have a place just like this in a month or so!" said Kelly Kelliher. "Isn't that exciting! I bet you can't wait!"

I tried to smile.

What I *couldn't wait* for, was to get the heck out of this place.

TEN

Getting ready in the mornings took forever now that I had to mess with this stupid haircut. I missed the simple ponytail days but would never give my mom the satisfaction of knowing that. By the time I straightened my bangs and gelled and clipped the rest of it into submission, I was almost late to school. I walked as quickly as I could to my locker, to drop off some of the more ridiculously heavy books. When I shut my locker door, Derek's face appeared out of nowhere.

"Hey," he said.

It was like I'd fallen off a jungle gym and had the air knocked out of me. I fought to catch my breath and forced a smile, saying, "Hey."

"There's a party at Greg's house this weekend, you should go." It was not a question. I held my binder like a shield.

"Cool," I said. I could feel a drop of sweat running down

my spine, a dull needle. I tried to remember who Greg was, not that it mattered.

"All right, well, see ya later." He jerked his head a little to the side to get a swipe of bangs out of his eyes, a move an eighth grader might make, and I tried not to swoon. He turned and was swallowed up by the moving crowd of kids.

It was unfathomable to me that I had become one of those girls who had a cute boy come up to their locker and say stuff like that to them.

It was a science day, so I hurried off to Mr. Lee's class.

Instead of his usual uniform of khakis, a light blue shirt, and some sort of science-themed tie, Mr. Lee was wearing a green T-shirt that said, PEOPLE ARE OK, BUT I PREFER BUGS! Insects formed the letters of the word BUGS. The room was filled with the random sounds of notebooks being plopped on desks, the unzipping of backpacks, and the barely audible sighs of a bunch of kids resigning themselves to the fact that they had to start trying to pay attention to something boring.

But Mr. Lee had a look of excitement that I hadn't seen when we were talking about biomes last week. Some people were murmuring about what a weirdo he was when he suddenly jumped up onto his chair, crouching and holding the front of it with his hands. His eyes were big as he peered out at us and waited for us to stop laughing and calm down.

"One day, insects will inherit the world!" he said in a booming voice. He climbed down from his chair. He had gotten our attention.

"Insects make up over seventy-five percent of all animal species. At any given moment there are an estimated ten *quintillion* insects crawling around this planet!" He wrote down the number ten followed by eighteen zeros. "They existed hundreds of millions of years *before* humanity. And if there's a zombie apocalypse, they'll *still* be around when the rest of us are just lunch!"

"Yeah," said one of the makeup girls. "But they're disgusting." A couple of people laughed.

"I had a feeling you'd say that," said Mr. Lee. He turned on the SMART Board and an image came up of a neon-green beetle with luminescent purple spots. Underneath the shell, its belly was glowing in a thousand different colors, blending seamlessly from orange into a deep reddish purple. Each leg was bright turquoise and melded into an inky dark green. The whole thing was shining like it was made up of precious jewels. There were some whispery oohs bubbling up from the room.

He turned to the next slide. The screen was covered in big blue-green ovals that looked like they had been painted and then outlined in thick black marker. There were orange squiggles outlining the black. The camera pulled back and it was a bug, its shell like a painted fingernail. "This is called *Sphaerocoris annulus* or a Picasso bug."

I couldn't believe something in nature was crawling around looking like a tiny painting. This was definitely not your average cockroach.

"And there's a reason these bugs are such beautiful colors. We've talked about adaptation in this class. Can anyone tell me what adaptation is?"

The whole room was quiet, everyone still staring at the screen.

"Anyone?" His hands were on his hips as he searched the room for a sign of intelligence.

"If you were a tiny bug and almost *everything* was trying to eat you, what could you do? You're just a bug!"

"Shoot poisonous daggers at it through my eyes," said Dylan Taylor. Mr. Lee darted a quick look over at Dylan without moving his head. I'm sure he was wondering if it might be a good idea to get the guidance counselor down here with a straitjacket.

"There are plenty of bugs that don't have that capability," he said calmly. He decided not to take any more chances asking us for ideas.

"Well, one of the ingenious ways that some bugs have figured out how to *not* be breakfast is by turning into a kaleidoscope of colors that make predators think, 'That can't be food. It looks like something from another planet! It must be poisonous!'"

He picked up a sandwich that was sitting on his desk. "If

this thing was glowing purple and orange, it would be beautiful, but I don't think I'd put it in my mouth? Would you?"

Some people gave a slight laugh and this little bit of encouragement got him going. "Insects also have skeletons on the outside of their body, called exoskeletons, like this pill bug." He showed us a picture of a not-so-beautiful grayish thing that looked like it was covered in armor like a medieval knight. "There are even insects that have figured out how to use their victims as camouflage!" He showed an image of something that we could barely see under a mass of ant carcasses.

"Ewwww . . . ," said a few people. I agreed. Totally disgusting, but definitely brilliant.

"Insects have developed thousands of unique ways to adapt to their environments in order to survive and they'll continue to do that long after we're gone. Basically, bugs are . . . *dope!*" He attempted some sort of "gangster" move with his hands.

And just like that, he lost us.

When it was finally time to see Lotti at lunch, I had to stop myself from running to our table in the corner of the cafeteria. Instead, I looked like one of those speed-walking weirdos, robotic from the waist up, holding my tray completely still, and a cartoon character from the waist down, my hips moving frantically back and forth as I tried to walk as fast as possible. I was weaving and dodging through people, like I was on hot sand. Lotti tried not to spit out her mac and cheese when she saw me beelining it right toward her. Seeing her smiling face was like spotting land after being lost at sea. She was a beautiful tropical island . . . with dark wavy hair.

"Oh my god, why are you walking that way?" she said through a giggle.

"Because!" I said, bulging my eyes at her, trying not to shout, ". . . There was an *incident*!" I launched into a detailed play-by-play of what had happened at my locker. Derek's little head toss as he whipped his hair around, the prickly feeling all over my skin as I tried to stay conscious and not look like a complete loser.

"Oh my god, he invited you to a party?" asked Lotti.

"*Invited* is a strong word," I said. "He basically just told me about it, like, 'For your information Greg is having a party, goodbye.' But he didn't say goodbye. He just walked away."

"Duh, he wants you to go!" she scream-whispered.

"I'm not going anywhere without you," I said.

"Of course not." She grabbed my hand. The two of us were almost floating, like someone had put helium in our chocolate milk.

ELEVEN

Thursday night after dinner my mom asked me to go down to the basement and help my dad go through some old baby stuff. I got a little adrenaline rush as the squeaky steps reminded me to be slightly afraid of this damp space whose corners were always dark. The pathetic attempt of a single bulb hanging from the middle of the room did very little to make it less creepy.

"Hey sunshine," said my dad, turning to see me.

"I'm supposed to help you get rid of stuff," I said.

"Well you're probably not very qualified for that job, given the state of your room." He winked, and I stuck my tongue out at him. We both smiled.

He was holding a brightly colored plastic saucer about the size of a small sled. There was a tray perched above it with bright yellow springy legs. It had all kinds of random colorful toys stuck to it.

"When you were tiny you used to spend hours in this thing," my dad said, putting it on the floor by my feet.

I squatted next to it and pictured myself as a baby, my chubby little fingers pushing pointless buttons and spinning the rattly tubes whose multicolored beads made a crackling sound. There was an alligator whose body was made up of little piano keys and when I pressed one it played a few notes of some nursery rhyme over and over again. There was a purple elephant head with googly eyes, that watched from its perch. It looked scared. And why wouldn't it be? This thing was bound to drive anyone nuts. The whole contraption must've been my command central and I was a bouncing, drooling, button-pushing, one-baby show.

"You couldn't get enough of this thing," said Dad.

"I'm sure it drove you and Mom crazy," I said, having a staring contest with the elephant.

"Are you kidding me? We could sit, totally sleep-deprived, and watch you entertain yourself. It was the best! I think this thing saved my sanity. Maybe we should take it to the new house, you know, in case you get bored."

"Ha ha," I said.

He ruffled my hair, something I only let *him* do, and started back in on the pile of plastic.

"You were quite a cutie," he said. There was a look in his eyes that made it seem like he'd rather be somewhere else.

I thought about how much easier life must've been as a baby, bouncing up and down, pushing a bunch of buttons, and I wondered if my dad was thinking the same thing. He didn't really know me these days.

"When you were little, I used to carry you around the house making the goofy noises from the *Seinfeld* theme song, it would keep you perfectly satisfied for hours."

He started making popping sounds with his lips, moving his head back and forth. I laughed. It was hard to imagine there was a time when this was all I needed to be completely content, being wrapped in my dad's arms, watching him make funny faces and ridiculous noises.

Now it was more complicated.

I thought about Derek, staring at me in class, appearing out of nowhere at my locker, asking me to go to some party. This stuff was supposed to make me happy. And part of me *was* happy. It felt good to get attention from a boy. It was like the adrenaline rush of the creaky basement stairs—something exciting might happen! Maybe even something scary! But at the same time, there was another part of me that just wanted to crawl into my dad's muscly arms and listen to him sing.

"Well, you're still a cutie to me," he said. "Let's get out of this basement and go get some ice cream."

"Good idea," I said, and I hugged him. I raced up the stairs toward the kitchen, not even hearing the squeaky step.

TWELVE

Staring at a blank sheet of paper, it was hard to keep my mind from wandering as I sat in study hall. I was supposed to be working on my essay about *Lord of the Flies*. Ms. Binney's assignment read, *How does Ralph represent civilization? What does Piggy represent?*

These kinds of questions always made my brain empty itself of any intelligent thought. All I could think was, *They both represent how completely unreadable this book is to anyone who isn't a bloodthirsty moron.*

Despite the quiet of the library, somehow Derek was able to sneak up on me.

"Hey," he said.

"Oh, hey," I said, trying to quickly recover from a minor heart attack.

"What are you working on?" He sat himself down. *Oh,*

okay, I thought. *I guess he's staying.* He smelled like gasoline and fabric softener. I assumed this was a combination of his parents and started to form a picture of his house in my head.

"The paper we have to write for Ms. Binney," I said. "But I'm kind of stuck."

"Well, you're really smart. You'll figure it out," he said through his gummy smile. He reached over and stroked my shoulder. I felt every muscle in my body roll out from that touch like rippling waves.

I smiled.

"I don't know, a bunch of boys running around on an island trying to kill each other? Not really my thing." I was trying to ignore the fact that his hand was still sitting on my shoulder. Being touched by someone I barely knew was setting my skin on fire.

"What they needed was a hot girl like you to set them straight."

I heard a giggle come out of my mouth and for a second I forgot that I hated the sound of girls giggling.

"You coming to the party this weekend?" he asked me, tilting his head.

"Yeah, I guess," I said. In my brain I repeated the mantra *Play it cool, Greta, play it cool*. "Can I bring my friend Lotti?"

"Is she the one with the dark hair and the braces?" he asked.

I nodded. "Yeah, she's, like, my best friend in the world."

As I said this, I saw Lotti's shiny metal smile coming toward me from the other side of the library.

I waved, trying my best not to run over and throw my arms around her.

I gave her a look that said *Come over here, now! I'm freaking out!* and she headed right to us.

"Hey!" she said. She was immediately shushed by the librarian.

"Sorry," she whispered.

I was just trying to unscramble my brain to figure out how to navigate talking to Lotti and Derek at the same time when I realized that I didn't have to. Derek was already getting up to leave.

"I gotta go, see ya at the party," he said. He slid out from the table and gave us a kind of a half wave as he casually walked away.

Lotti gave me that look that said *Tell me every single detail about what's going on*.

When I told her about the "hot girl" comment, her mouth dropped open. But nothing prepared her for the next part of the story . . . *the shoulder.*

"Are you kidding me?!" asked Lotti, looking like she was trying with every fiber of her being to not explode in the middle of the library.

"It was . . . weird," I said. And as meaningless as that word can be, I couldn't think of another way to describe it. It was just about impossible these days to figure out when I was terrified and when I was extremely happy (although I don't think there have been many extremely happy moments). Both emotions were so busy coursing through my entire body that they never seemed to make it to my brain, where I could untangle what was happening.

Lotti came around the table and sat where Derek had been sitting. When our legs touched, I was able to take my first deep breath of the day.

"You're definitely coming to this party with me," I said, grabbing one of her hands and holding it in both of mine like it was a secret treasure. Which it was.

THIRTEEN

Convincing my mom to let me go to the party wasn't as hard as I thought it would be. I got the usual question: "Will a parent be there?"

I had no idea, but I gave my usual answer: "Of course."

When I told her that Lotti's mom had said yes, it sealed the deal. The two of them were equally suspicious of all activities. Lotti and I called them the Worriers. Sometimes it seemed like all the other kids were living with parents who were basically just their roommates. They were allowed to do anything. I pictured the makeup girls *telling . . . not asking*, their moms about the party. I've seen moms like this in their giant SUVs at pickup. They looked like older versions of their daughters, wearing the same clothes and layers of makeup, desperate to be seen as cool, terrified of their understandably scary daughters' dismissive eye rolls.

But not Maggie Goodwin. My mom considered every event or activity that needed her permission like she was an FBI agent and we were in a cinder block–walled interrogation room.

And who, exactly, is *this* Greg? I pictured her asking. *And remember, everything you say can and will be used against you!*

But this time my mom was so busy wrestling with the plastic packing tape on the seventeenth box she'd packed that day that she let her guard down.

"Well, I guess so," she said over the screech of the tape. "If Lotti's mom said yes. I will be texting her to confirm that." She gave me a warning look through an annoying strand of hair before she blew it out of her face.

"Yup," I said, and I quickly ran up to my room to call Lotti.

"My mom's texting your mom to make sure that she said yes, so . . ." I was afraid to get too excited before we worked this thing out. It could get tricky.

"I told *my* mom that *your* mom said yes, too," said Lotti, giving me a nervous look through FaceTime.

"Uh-oh. Well, it's all up to the party gods now. My mom is pretty distracted these days with the big move to the fake house, so who knows how much she's actually paying attention," I said, crossing my fingers and biting my bottom lip.

"Oh my god, Greta. We're going to our first middle school party!" Her eyes were beaming with excitement and she put all her fingertips in her mouth. "What are you going to wear?"

I saw myself in the small rectangle at the bottom of the screen. "I don't know, but you have to help me with this stupid hair." I pulled at it like I was trying to take off a wig. "Ugh."

"Well, obviously Derek doesn't think it's stupid," she said with an exaggerated wink.

"That seems literally impossible," I said. "But maybe."

My mom having done a minimal amount of detective work because she was totally off her game, and because Lotti's mom *Didn't want to bother Maggie, she's so stressed out these days* . . .

The Worriers agreed to let us go.

Lotti and I had decided on matching outfits. I think we were using the same logic that our elementary school teachers used on class trips: *If you're dressed in the same shirts, you won't get lost.*

We chose the tank tops we'd gotten at the store together, Lotti's sophisticated black bra strap peeking out from under hers. Mine was a slight variation. Instead of people seeing my immature white strap, I just layered another black tank top underneath mine.

Voilà. Problem solved.

We both wore our best jeans, and Lotti had worked on my hair for an hour.

"Wow, it's pretty out here," Mom said as she drove us

down Greg's long driveway. "And his parents are home, right?" she asked the rearview mirror.

"Yes, Mom," I said, rolling my eyes at Lotti.

"So this Greg, he's a friend of yours? Is he nice?" She snuck a look at me in the rearview mirror that meant *Wink wink, is this a potential boyfriend?*

"He's just some kid we know," I said. This was only partially true. If I had to pick Greg out of a lineup of five thirteen-year-old boys with brown hair and bad skin, I'd have trouble.

As we pulled up to the house, we saw a bunch of other cars parked in Greg's driveway. Through the lit windows we could see lots of grown-ups talking to each other and laughing, so Mom decided it was okay to not take this opportunity to publicly humiliate me by insisting on a formal introduction to Greg's mother. "All right, girls, I'll be back to pick you up at ten," she said. She tried to give me a look that said something predictable like *Make good choices.* But I was already halfway out of the car.

FOURTEEN

Greg's mom staggered a little as she opened the door, looking at someone behind her. She barely registered our presence. Her bracelets were jangling like yappy little dogs each time she moved her hand, which held a glass of pinkish wine that was dangerously close to sloshing onto her white sweater.

"Greggy's in the basement, go ahead down, girls," she said, waving her hand at us like we were insects. I was very glad that my mom had broken character and not insisted on meeting this woman. She would not approve. Between the drinking and the fact that she seemed completely oblivious to what her son was doing, unsupervised, with a bunch of kids in a dark basement? Well, let's just say there would have been a "change of plans," and it would have turned into game night at my house with Fej and my dad.

Lotti and I walked quickly through the grown-up party where everyone was too loud and sloppy. I felt like we were being buckled into a roller coaster by a monkey. We were on our own, so we'd better hold on tight.

When we got to the basement there were only seven kids there. The mood was very different from the mood upstairs. A deep bass tumbled out of a speaker and seemed to flatten everyone against the dingy furniture.

"Whassup?" said Greg, with a nod of acknowledgment.

Lotti and I stood there like conjoined twins. "Hey," we said in unison.

Everyone went back to what they were doing before we came in. Which, as far as I could tell, was nothing. They were staring at their phones and their expressionless faces glowed in the dimly lit room like they were bodiless creatures, floating in the dank basement air. Two boys were sitting completely still in front of a video game. The only sign that they weren't mannequins was the way their fingers frantically swarmed around their game consoles.

Lotti and I found an armchair that we both squeezed into. Two of the makeup girls were laughing about something, and I did my best to not assume it was me. I reached up and felt the bumps of the twelve hair clips that were doing their best to contain my curls.

"Evan's here," Lotti whispered in my ear. Since there were only seven other people in the room this was not news to me.

"Don't leave me," I whispered, slightly growling.

We sat perfectly still, like we were waiting for someone to tell us what to do, Lotti biting her lips and trying not to let out a squeal. I tried to act casual while she squeezed the blood out of my hand.

Since nobody else was talking to us, Lotti and I just went along like we usually did. She quietly whispered random observations into my ear ("Isn't that girl an eighth grader?" "It smells like my grandfather in here." "I like Evan's shirt.") and I tried to pay attention while scanning the room for whatever might be coming next.

Over Lotti's shoulder I saw Evan S. making his way to our flower-upholstered lifeboat. In my best ventriloquist voice, I smiled and whispered, "Evan S. is coming over." She squeezed so hard I thought she might break my hand.

"Hey," he said. "I didn't know you'd be here."

"Oh, hey," answered Lotti, trying with every fiber of her being to play it cool.

"Hi Evan," I said, waving. He barely registered my existence and kept smiling at Lotti.

I know that everyone has their own taste, but I did not see what Lotti saw in Evan S. First of all, he's short. Lotti's pretty tall and although I've never seen them stand next to each other, I'm almost positive that Evan would have to look up into Lotti's nostrils when they were talking. Plus, Evan's obsessed with sports. I've only ever seen him in some kind of team jersey. It's weird to me that he's constantly walking around with someone else's name on his back. But, whatever. Lotti thinks he's awesome.

I was just in the process of convincing myself that my best friend wasn't in love with a doofus when I registered that she was unwedging herself from our chair. She looked like someone trying to get out of an inner tube and onto a dock. It is not something that can be done gracefully. She finally popped out and I felt unanchored and alone.

"I'm gonna go get something to eat with Evan, I'll be right back." She gave me a don't-worry smile but I still started to panic.

I looked around the dimly lit room, making sure I didn't make eye contact with anyone. I pretended to not hate the music, which was at least loud enough that it gave me a good excuse not to talk. The singer was mumbling angrily about something over a beat that was begging us to pretend we were in some sort of club and not Greg's mostly brown basement.

One of the makeup girls came over to me.

"Hey, didn't you use to have really long hair?" Not sure where this could possibly go as a topic of conversation, I just said, "Yeah."

"It was so pretty!" she cooed.

I shrugged.

"I mean, it looks really good now, too!" She reached over and touched one of my clear hair clips. There was a silence that I assumed meant that we were going to switch to a more interesting subject, but no.

This girl knew more about hair and haircut-related subject matter than I ever would in my entire lifetime.

The next fifteen minutes were a blur of me trying to feign interest in what Makeup was saying while sneaking looks for Lotti over her shoulder.

"So, I think I'm gonna like, shave underneath and keep it long on top." She looked at me, holding up her stringy blond hair on top of her head. I guess that she was waiting for a response. I thought about the dramatic scene I had to perform just to get my mom to let me cut mine. If the word *shave* had been in that scenario, she'd probably *still* be screaming at me.

"That'll be cool," I said. "Do you know where the bathroom is?" She pointed up the stairs toward the grown-up nonsense that was even louder than when we first got there.

I took the long way around the room so I could look for Lotti. The basement was dark and full of old workout equipment and Christmas decorations. It was hard to decipher what was a person and what was junk. But there, crammed in the corner of one of the couches, was a creature made up of Lotti and Evan. They were all over each other. Just as I predicted, if that kid had opened his eyes while he slobbered on my best friend, he would have gotten a good look up her nose.

I think my jaw dropped open. So much for playing it cool.

Suddenly I felt sweaty and light-headed. "Lotti! Can I talk to you for a minute?" I said, a little too loudly and a little too much like my mother.

Startled, she looked up at me with Evan's slobber ringing her mouth. It was disgusting.

"What?" she asked.

"It's really important that I talk to you in private right this second," I said, my eyes straining to open as wide as possible so Lotti could read my face.

"Fine. Evan, I'll be right back," she said, untangling herself from the squat little limbs in the oversize football jersey.

"Cool," he said.

"Hey Evan," I said casually.

"Hey," he said, barely looking at me.

I dragged Lotti to another dark corner of the basement, over by a dusty treadmill. We sat on the rubber tread, and I started in on her.

"Oh my god, what are you doing? You said you wouldn't leave me!" I was whispering as angrily as I could.

"Greta, are you serious? You know how much I like Evan, you can't be mad. You should be happy for me!"

Lotti and I have only fought twice since first grade. Once was when I cut the sleeves off one of her favorite shirts that I had borrowed. (My bad.)

And the other time was when she told her mom that I was the one who broke a ceramic green tiger that had been her grandmother's. (We were playing queen of the jungle and things got a little heated. Who can remember who broke what?)

But this was different. A boy was coming between us. This was not supposed to happen.

Up until tonight, I had never felt lonely when I was around Lotti. It didn't matter what we were doing. She was my soulmate. Nothing made me feel safer and more alive than when she was with me, and I could smell the beeswax soap she used to wash her face and hear her snort when she was trying not to laugh out loud. But sitting next to her on this machine someone had gotten years ago with the hope of a better, healthier life, that now sat useless and ignored, made my eyes start to sting.

I didn't want to cry in front of all these people. "Whatever, Lotti. I need to get some air," I said, marching to the sliding glass doors.

I hadn't realized how hot it was in the basement until I felt the cool, clean night air on my face. I took a deep stuttering breath and closed my eyes, listening to the katydids chirping in the darkness. I tried not to cry. There was no moon, and without it the sky was dark and opaque.

I felt someone coming up behind me. It was Derek.

"Hey," he said. He was cuter in the dark. His hands were shoved in his pockets, and he looked at me like he was a little nervous. It softened me toward him and I started to talk.

"Lotti and I just got in a huge fight," I said. He didn't say anything, so I kept going, describing the deceit and treachery that I had just endured. When it looked like I was finished talking, he shrugged.

"That sucks," he said.

Wiser words were never spoken, Derek, I thought.

"It does indeed suck," I said.

He coughed up a half-hearted laugh and reached over and took one of my hands that had been tightly gripping my sides against the cool night air.

His hand was warm from being in his pocket.

Okay, I thought. *This isn't so bad. Derek's kind of sweet, he's there for me when I really need him.* I tried to relax into the moment. I was holding hands with Derek like we were a couple, and we started to walk toward the edge of the yard.

"Greg's mom seems nice," I said, trying to make conversation. Because nothing says casual and flirty like bringing up someone's mother. Ugh.

"She's a train wreck," said Derek. "She's totally wasted. Greg tries to just ignore her."

This seemed like a pretty accurate description, and I had sudden sympathy for Greg. I was about to say something when I felt the rough snag of tree bark on the back of my shirt.

"You look really hot tonight," he breathed inches from my face.

"Thanks," I said. "So do you." I was not good at this, but apparently Derek didn't notice, because he leaned in closer and closed his eyes. *This is it!* I thought. My first real kiss! I closed my eyes and felt Derek's smooth cheek when he pressed his face against mine. It felt completely bizarre to have someone else's lips pressed against mine, like he was an alien. An alien with very thin dry lips. I could smell soap. He had washed his face just for this moment, I thought. *Just for me. He really cares about me, I'm not totally alone without Lotti! Someone else cares about me!* Not knowing what to do with my hands at this point, I casually draped them around his neck, pretty sure I had seen people do that when they kissed.

Suddenly his gummy mouth was pressing hard against my lips, and his teeth knocked against mine making me aware of the skull beneath my skin. "Ow," I said, hoping this would break him from the trance he was in. "Sorry," he said, smirking a little. But he kept going. I felt his muscly little tongue trying to pry my mouth open and the chemical smell of Doritos mixed with saliva almost made me retch. I needed to get some air. I tried to move away but his knee was pressed between my legs, holding me against the rough bark of the tree. It was poking into the skin of my lower back where my shirt had gotten bunched up. His hands were like rodents crawling all over my body and I lost track of where I was. He had gotten under my shirt and was pulling at my bra. I used both of my hands to yank his arm out, but he slid from my grasp and went for the button of my jeans. I was suddenly in a nightmare that I couldn't wake myself up from. It seemed like I was being held there by more than one person (it had to be!) and before I knew what was happening, he had ahold of my hand and was forcing it against the crotch of his jeans. I jerked my hand away and pushed Derek's chest as hard as I could.

"What?" he said. He looked genuinely confused.

"Just stop, okay?" I said, trying to control the panic in my voice. "Can we just slow down?" Derek had suddenly transformed into someone very different from the sweet boy who was holding my hand not even five minutes ago. But he wasn't listening. He pushed against me again and I started swatting at his arms as they tried to force their way back underneath my clothes.

"Get off!" I said with the little bit of air that was left in my lungs. I had been holding my breath in terror.

I pushed as hard as I could and broke free. I ran the fifty feet back to the basement, which felt like it was miles away. I pulled back the sliding glass door and scanned the room for Lotti.

She was back with Evan on the couch and when our eyes met, the smile disappeared from her face.

"Greta?" she said. I grabbed her hand and pulled her up

the basement stairs. Some of the grown-ups were dancing like idiots. The men with their "white man's overbite" moves, elbows clamped against their sweaters as they jerkily moved their shoulders back and forth. The women were shaking their Sydney Coorly–size chests so hard it looked painful. Everyone was way too loud.

I finally found a bathroom and we locked the door. There was nowhere to sit so we both climbed into the bathtub. I immediately curled up against Lotti's shoulder and started to cry.

"What happened?" said Lotti, stroking my hair, which was no longer pressed safely against my head. It was wild now and sprang in different directions, hectic and confused.

I couldn't talk. I couldn't find words to tell my best friend what had happened. All I could do was try, in that moment, to get back into the body that had been taken from me so roughly. Pawed at, reshaped into something I didn't recognize.

When I didn't answer, she stopped asking and just started rocking us gently.

After a few minutes, she whispered into the top of my head, "Was it Derek? Did something happen?"

I nodded, my face still buried against her shirt.

She pulled a piece of bark out of my hair and smoothed the fear out of my curls. She kissed the top of my head. "He's such a weasel," she said. "I'm gonna kill him." She got her phone out of her back pocket. "I'm texting your mom to come get us."

I hugged her tighter, and we stayed in the tub until my mom wrote back.

FIFTEEN

When my mom pulled up, we were waiting in the driveway so she wouldn't go inside. "Hi Mrs. G.," said Lotti as we climbed into the back seat and tried to act as normal as possible. Luckily for me, it was not out of character to answer my mom's storm of questions with one-word answers.

"Did you have fun?"

"Yep."

"Were there a lot of kids there?"

"Nope."

"Were Greg's parents nice?"

"Sure."

"What did you do?"

"Nothing."

Lotti, who was unbelievably good at the whole parent-talk

thing, changed the subject by asking my mom if she had had a nice night, too.

My mom was completely helpless when confronted with extreme politeness. She fell for it every time. She started talking about some movie she and my dad had watched about a man and woman who fell in love but couldn't be together until they were old. The woman got Alzheimer's and fell in love with the man every time she saw him, like they'd never met, like he was a stranger.

"Oh, we've seen it a thousand times." She sighed. "But it's great. It's so romantic. Every time I watch it, I think, now that's the way you tell a love story."

I could feel Lotti looking at me as I stared out the window. She squeezed my hand tight, knowing it was taking every ounce of courage I had not to break into a million pieces.

"Sounds great, Mrs. G.," she said. My mom kept talking, describing scenes where the man would visit the woman in a nursing home when they were old. He'd play her their favorite song, which she had forgotten, and ask her to dance.

"That's so sad," said Lotti.

My mom dropped Lotti off at her house and I pretended to be asleep in the back seat. When we pulled into the driveway, she shut off the car and nudged my arm.

"Sweetie, we're home," she whispered. My whole body

wanted to grab my mother and never let her go. I wanted to tell her how sorry I was that I even went to that party. How I never wanted to go anywhere, ever again. I wanted her to hold me and tell me that everything was going to be all right. That I didn't have to get any older if I didn't want to. I could stay with her in our house forever. That I'd always be safe.

Instead, I just looked at her.

We sat in silence for a second. Then she wound her pinkie around mine and I almost started to cry. "Thanks for picking us up," I said, and I opened the door and went inside.

My dad was snoring in front of the TV. I said, "'Night" in the most chipper voice I could muster as I ran up the stairs to my room.

I quickly took off my clothes that smelled like stale basement air and sap. I winced as I touched the scrapes on my back made by the bark of the tree. My whole body felt limp, my muscles starting to unclench for the first time in hours. I closed my eyes as I wrapped myself in the soft fleece of my pajamas, which had the slightly sour smell of my skin from this morning.

When I was different.

When I was myself.

I got under the covers and curled into a ball.

I didn't want to close my eyes. I didn't want to replay what happened with Derek over and over again in my mind.

The light from the street lit my room just enough for me to see the clutter all around me, like a nest.

My mom's fingernails tapped on my door.

Her voice was soft coming from the other side. "Greta, are you all right, honey?"

How could I possibly answer that question? None of me was right. The whole world had changed, gotten dirtier and unfamiliar. I tightened the curl of my body under the covers until my knees touched my chest. They felt like someone else's knees, and I winced. I turned over and faced the window next to my bed. The sky was full of smoky-looking clouds and seemed to close down over the world. I felt claustrophobic.

"Yeah, I'm just tired," I said, trying to sound casual. "Good night, Mom."

"Okay. I love you, sweetie," she said.

I didn't know if she left or was still standing on the other side of the door. But she didn't say anything else after that.

SIXTEEN

When I woke up the next morning, it took me a few seconds to realize that what had happened the night before was not just a nightmare. I stared at a blank section of my wall and tried to force my body into recognition. Nothing about me physically had actually changed, yet I felt different, like my blood had gotten thicker. Like it was taking up more space in my body, leaving less room to breathe.

I went and sat in front of my mirror. My eyes looked . . . bulgy. I know Lotti always says I don't have the best self-image, that I don't really see myself clearly. But when I looked closer it seemed like my eyes were bigger. Either that or my head had gotten smaller. My hair was still wild from the night before and I wondered where I had left all my hair clips.

That must be it, I thought. *Bigger hair, smaller-looking head.*

Like one of those chickens that looks like it's wearing a troll doll wig. Lovely.

I curled up on the floor with my phone, looking up *What causes googly eyes?* when there was a sudden knocking on my door that made me jump.

"Go away," I snarled.

"Good morning to you, too, sunshine," said my dad. "Breakfast."

I rubbed my eyes hard, hoping that maybe they just needed a good push back into my head and I went down to eat.

Fej was drumming on boxes like it was the middle of the afternoon and not morning when some of us were trying to just get some cereal and avoid all human contact.

"Can you stop that? You're such a pain," I growled at him, my face only inches away from my Cheerios, a decadence we were only allowed to have on the weekend. I had covered them in a crystally layer of sugar.

"Well, someone woke up on the wrong side of the bed," said my mom as she scrolled through her phone. "What's your plan today, Greta?" she asked. God forbid a weekend should go by without every moment scheduled with *productive* activities.

"I don't know. I'll probably hang out with Lotti." I slurped my milk, which is the same thing as letting out a huge burp as far as my mom is concerned. She glared at me.

"Well, at some point I want you to pack up that room of yours. As far as I can tell, you haven't even started."

I ignored her.

After a few minutes of nothing but the sound of Fej drumming insanely on boxes and the clang of my spoon against my bowl as I tried to get every drop of the milk at the bottom, the wet sugar settled underneath it like sweet sand, my mom put down her phone. I felt her looking at me.

"What?" I said.

"I was thinking it might be a good day for you and me to go see the new house! It's not quite finished so you'll have to picture what it'll look like once all our stuff is moved in. We could go out to lunch, too! There's a great little salad place near the new neighborhood, it'll be fun! We'll make a day of it."

Salad *and* a tour of a house I don't want anything to do with? She must've read my mind!

I gave her a look that said *Please don't do this*.

She cupped my face in her palm and gave me an encouraging smile.

Up close like this, she seemed to notice that something about me looked different.

"Everything okay, sweetie? You feeling all right?" she asked me, tilting her head.

I didn't want to make eye contact so close, afraid she might see a change in me, and I broke away from her hand.

"Just super excited about the salad," I said, the sarcasm working exactly as I'd hoped. She sat back in her chair and picked up her phone.

There was something about being in the passenger seat when my mom was driving that made me feel trapped. I was completely at her mercy. If she wanted to go on twelve different errands "while we were out" there was nothing I could do about it. Never mind any protests of "Mom, c'mon, let's just go home." It was like we were pioneer people on a wagon who had to ride miles to get to the nearest form of civilization. Everything had to be done on this journey. Who knew when we'd be able to get to town again.

I stayed in the car while she went into Target to "pick up a few things." I looked at myself in the side-view mirror. *Objects may appear closer than they actually are* was written on the bottom. *Well, I hope so*, I thought. *I looked small and so far away.*

I had a flash of the night before, of Derek's face smashed into mine. I felt his hands grabbing at my clothes. I shook my head and sent a text to Lotti.

Hey

Hey
What's up?

> Just sitting prisoner in the target parking lot while my mother buys crap she doesn't need. You?

Just woke up.

You ok?

It was a question that I had no idea how to answer. At some point I'd have to tell Lotti what had happened. But first I had to answer that for myself. Telling her, *He kissed me and grabbed at me*, didn't sound like enough. It was more than that. There was nothing like affection or warmth in Derek's hands. They were aggressive and chaotic. We weren't making out. It was a fight for possession of my body, and I just barely won.

> Yeah. I'll call ya later.

My mom opened the tailgate and put a bunch of junk in the back. "Let's go see the new house!" she said, beaming.

I sent Lotti a picture of my snarling face, my fingers making a gun to my forehead.

> Now she's taking me to Beigeville

?????

The new house.

Worst.

Day.

Ever.

"So, did you and Lotti have fun last night?" my mom asked, keeping her eyes on the road.

"Yeah, it was fine," I said.

This was her second attempt to get something out of me and when it didn't work, she switched on the radio. An Elton John song was playing, and my mom sang along at the top of her lungs, deliberately messing up the words. "Rocket man, bringin' home a ham and provolone!"

She looked over at me and smiled. I tried to keep my lips perfectly neutral, but I couldn't help but grin . . . a little.

When we pulled into the driveway of the new house, my stomach tightened into a ball, like a frightened hedgehog. The giant arched windows looked cold and mean. They seemed to be sneering at me. *Don't even* think *about singing or laughing when you get in here. This place is for quiet contemplation and adult dinner parties with boring people only.*

My mom struggled to get the right key while she juggled the stuff she'd gotten out of the back of the car.

"Greta, go get the new welcome mat I bought, it's in the back of the car."

This house does not *need a welcome mat*, I thought. *Maybe a* Here is where dreams go to die *mat. Or a* Hope you like soulless, empty spaces *mat.*

When we shut the door behind us, the sound echoed like we were in a dungeon. My mom started twirling around with her hands outstretched. "Oh there's so much room! I can breathe! And look at all the light!"

From where I stood, I could see nothing but beige walls and cold tile floors. It felt like we were the first human beings to set foot in this place. Without the random knickknacks and cookie-scented candle, it seemed like an institution.

"Your room is at the top of the stairs to the left." She couldn't stop smiling.

When I got to "my room" it looked like everything else, beige. The upstairs was covered in carpet that was . . . you guessed it, beige. I tried to imagine all my stuff in here. My posters and books, my old stuffed animals and Christmas lights. But every time I pictured something of mine in this space, the walls would just absorb it like some sort of giant creature. I felt sadder the longer I stood there.

My mom came up behind me.

"Isn't it huge?" she asked, putting an arm around my shoulder.

"Yup. It's like a huge empty warehouse," I said. My sarcasm seemed to deflate my mom into a wilted balloon, and I immediately felt sorry.

"It's really bright," I said, trying to get on board.

"You're gonna love it, Greta. You'll see. Check out the bathroom, it's all yours! Well, yours and Jeffrey's, but still!" She gave me a squeeze and went back downstairs.

I went into the sterile bathroom and switched on the fluorescent light above the mirror. It made my skin a dead yellowish color. But that wasn't the only thing that looked wrong. For a second I didn't even recognize myself. Everything was just a little off. My eyes were still bulgy, and the rest of me looked smaller. *It must be this house*, I thought. It makes everything in it seem tiny. I went back downstairs to my mother. But she looked normal. Nothing about her looked different at all.

SEVENTEEN

When I saw Lotti at her locker Monday morning I hugged her, hard.

"Have you seen . . . him?" she whispered, scrunching up her face.

"No, but I have English today so I'm gonna have to be in the same room as him."

The bell rang for first period, and she squeezed my hand tight.

"See you at lunch," I said.

"It's gonna be okay, Greta," she said. We looked back at each other over our shoulders as we let the crowd take us in opposite directions.

When I walked into Ms. Binney's room for English and saw Derek sitting at a desk, I panicked. Flashes of his hands swarming my body came back to me and instead of taking a seat I went right up to Ms. Binney.

"I don't feel good," I said. "I need to go to the nurse." I gave her a look that implied that this was a woman emergency, and we didn't need to discuss it any further.

"Okay, don't forget the pass," she said, winking at me. I took the green lanyard with the laminated PASS sign off the hook next to her desk and hurried out the door.

When I got to the nurse's office, I grabbed at my lower stomach and did my best sick-person impression.

"Is it cramps, hun?" the nurse asked me through half-closed eyes. This was probably the most common thing she saw each day. She looked bored out of her mind. I nodded and sat on the gray vinyl-covered cot. Of course I didn't actually feel sick, but I didn't feel good either. I felt . . . different. It wasn't just my eyes. It seemed like after what happened at Greg's house that night, I had changed in a way I couldn't describe to Lotti or anyone else. I felt marked. Like Derek's hands had done something to my skin and everyone could see that something about me was wrong.

"Here, hun." The nurse handed me some ibuprofen and a plastic cup of water. She went back to her desk and plopped herself in front of her computer where she was losing at solitaire.

At lunch, Lotti was talking about Evan. Today he was wearing a LeBron James jersey that made his stubby little body look even more ridiculous. What was the point of this exactly? Did he think someone would be walking behind him and think, *Oh my god! I didn't know LeBron James went to this school!?*

Doofus.

"Do I look different to you?" I asked Lotti.

"What do you mean?" She squinted her eyes, concentrating hard on my face. "Did you get sunburned this weekend? I guess your skin's a little pinkish orange?" My mouth dropped open in horror and she immediately added, "But in a good way! I should lay out in the sun. I look gross." She stuck out her tongue and went back to her hockey-puck burger.

"I hardly even went outside this weekend," I said, touching my face.

After pushing my food around a little I looked at her. "I didn't go to English. I told Ms. Binney I had to go to the nurse. I couldn't be in the same room as Derek." Lotti gave me a sympathetic head tilt. She was waiting for more information.

"When you were with Evan at the party were you . . . scared?" I was practically whispering but she could hear me through the noise of the cafeteria. Lotti and I were on our own wavelength.

She seemed confused. "I mean it was exciting and kind of weird to be making out with someone, but I wouldn't say

I was *scared*." She got a dreamy look on her face as her mind wandered to her night on the couch with the doofus.

When she noticed that I was staring at my tray of food she reached over and grabbed my hand. "Are you going to tell me what happened with Derek?"

"It was *not* exciting," I said. I started rubbing my arms. My skin felt like it was squeezing my body, not just holding it all together, like it's supposed to. Maybe I did get sunburned over the weekend? Although I have no idea how.

Luckily, at dinner that night Fej had a lot to say about his day, so I was off the hook as far as talking.

"Sam Mackey fell off the jungle gym at recess and one of his teeth came out. There was blood all over his shirt. He looked like a vampire. It was awesome." He was shoveling mashed potatoes into his mouth while he talked and white goo was coming out the sides. He looked like a rabid dog.

"Don't talk with your mouth full, Jeffrey," my mom said, trying to ignore the bits of food stuck to his chin. She shot my dad a look and changed the subject. They started talking to each other about the new house. Words like *mortgage rates* and *closing costs* . . . It sounded like another language. Adult conversation is mind-numbingly boring. I don't know how they do it. I wondered at what point in their lives did they decide that it was time to only talk about grown-up nonsense. My mom has to have been an age when she would sit and talk with a friend about stupid stuff like hair and boys, but it's hard to believe. I tried to picture it. I got a ridiculous image in my head of my mother, as she looks right now, with her chin-length mom hair and her turtleneck, lying on her stomach on a rug, swinging her bent legs back and forth while she giggled with a middle school friend. It made me snort a stifled laugh. Unfortunately, this brought attention to me, and I heard my mom ask me a question.

"Are you feeling okay, Greta?" I didn't want to make eye contact, so I just stared at my mom's fork, still poised in midair.

"I don't know. Yeah, I guess so." I started rubbing my legs under the table. The tight feeling in my skin was getting worse.

"Your coloring looks . . . different. Do you have a fever?" Questions like this were always a good opportunity to get out of dinner and spend the rest of the night in my room. I might even be able to miss a day of school.

"Maybe," I said. I made my eyes a little droopy. "May I be excused? I think I want to go lie down."

"Of course, sweetie." My mom had that serious look on her face that was reserved for when her children were sick. "I'll be up in a minute to take your temperature."

"I wanna be excused, too!" said Fej, feeling the injustice of having to stay at the dinner table with his plate still full of wilted broccoli. "I'm really sick! I think I might be dying!" He grabbed at his throat and stuck out his tongue. In seconds he was lying on the floor groaning.

My dad pointed at Fej's plate with his fork. "Eat up, buddy. It's good for you. All the best baseball players eat broccoli." Fej let out a dramatic sigh and slid reluctantly back into his chair.

"I think I'm gonna just go to sleep," I said, letting the droopy act take over my whole body. "G'night." I consciously walked in a slow, I'm-so-sick way up to my room.

I kept the lights off as I scrolled through Instagram until I fell asleep.

EIGHTEEN

Some part of me knew I was dreaming.

I was running through the woods at night. I couldn't see him, but Derek was chasing me. I felt hands grabbing at the air just behind me. He had so many hands. I heard him grunting as he smashed through the leaves, getting closer. I tried to cry out, but I couldn't. I had no lips. Skin covered my mouth and bulged with the air from my muffled scream. I tripped on something, or maybe the leaves on the ground were hands, too? It slowed me down enough that I felt Derek grab hold of my shirt, pulling me back. I heard the high-pitched zippered tear of the fabric as it finally stretched too far and pulled loose from my body. The sting of the cold air on my skin pulled the breath out of my chest.

I woke up gasping. I had the sense of something tugging on me, like I had on a wet bathing suit . . . over my whole body. I felt like I was suffocating. It was so tight and the need to get it off me made me panic. A part of me realized that I was safe in my room, but I was still half asleep, and my bed was in the woods. The sky was getting brighter. My body felt like when I used to pour glue on my fingers and then peel it, trying to see how big a piece I could pull off. I started to tug on a flap by my ribs. When I got a good grasp I pulled slowly, feeling the release of the plasticky film. I kept pulling. The piece got larger and larger, and I wriggled and squirmed under the covers as I unpeeled what felt like the plastic coating on a Fruit Roll-Up from my body. My feet tugged and scraped at my legs, trying to pull it off. I could feel the weight of something sliding off me and I was finally free. There was something thin and rubbery against my toes. My whole body tingled at the touch of my warm sheets.

I was suddenly wide awake.

I threw open the blankets and looked down. At the bottom of the bed was what looked like a pinkish wadded-up wet suit. It was my skin. Or my old skin, I should say, because now . . . I was orange. Not the *Oh, you put on a lot of spray tan* kind of orange, but the actual *color* orange. I jumped out of bed and ran to the mirror. I looked like one of those crazy sports fans who paint their whole bodies to show just how dedicated they are to their team. I covered my mouth with my shaking hand so I wouldn't scream.

My heart was thumping hard against my chest as I

gathered up the sticky pile at the foot of my bed and stuffed it in the trash can in the corner. I stuck some papers and chip wrappers on top to cover it. I quickly threw the blankets over the damp sheets and sat down trying to catch my breath. There was no way I would be able to explain this to my mother. But I was scared and needed to make sure I was actually awake, that this was actually happening.

"*Mom!*" I yelled. "Can you come in here? *Now!*"

I heard her slippers shuffling quickly down the hallway.

She opened my door. "Oh my god," she said, putting her hands out as if to stop what was happening in front of her. "Greta! What have you done to yourself?!"

"I didn't do anything!" I yelled. "I woke up like this!"

"I need to call Dr. Saluja."

I stood shivering in my robe while my mom called the doctor. She reached out to touch me but pulled back, like she was afraid that whatever this was, it might be contagious.

NINETEEN

The paper that was covering the bed in Dr. Saluja's office felt rough on my skin, which was supersensitive and felt like it was slightly vibrating. When Dr. Saluja came into the room she tried to dampen her reaction. But in that split second before she was able to compose herself, I saw a look in her eyes that said *Holy crap*.

"Well, Greta. What seems to be going on?" she asked, taking in my orange body, which looked even brighter under the doctor's-office lights.

You're kidding, I thought. *What seems to be going on? How am I supposed to know?!*

"Um . . . well, I'm orange."

"I can see that. Have you started wearing any lotions or using any new soaps lately?"

"No."

"Has your diet changed?" She was staring at her laptop now as I answered her stupid questions. I think it was a lot easier than trying to look directly at me and pretend not to be horrified.

"You mean have I started to eat a ton of carrots and orange-flavored Jell-O? No."

My mom gave me a look that told me to stop being sarcastic. As if there was a proper way to act when you shed the skin from your entire body and turn bright orange.

"Have you used a self-tanning spray? Or gone to a tanning salon?"

"No!" I said.

She and my mom exchanged a look like I was lying to them.

"I didn't do anything! This just happened!" My voice was starting to get a little hysterical. I held out my arms in front of me, turning them like they were on a spit. Even my palms were orange.

"Okay, I'd like to do some tests. We're going to need to take some blood." Her eyes retreated to the safety of her laptop. "The nurse will be right in," she said, risking a quick peek in our direction.

When Dr. Saluja left the room, my mom turned to look at me.

"Are you sure there isn't something you're not telling me?" she asked.

I thought about the night of the party and my stomach clenched like a fist.

"Yes, Mom," I said with a sigh. "I'm sure."

There was a light knock on the door and a nurse with Minnie Mouse faces all over her uniform wheeled in a cart.

She wasn't quite as good at masking her amusement.

"Wowza! Someone went a little crazy with the tanning lotion, huh?!" She laughed, looking at my mom like, *Kids, am I right?* and prepared to poke me with needles.

By the end of the day, Dr. Saluja had done every test she could think of on me. Her verdict? I was perfectly healthy. She said there was nothing physically wrong with me and asked if perhaps I was under a lot of stress? *Uh, yes, Doctor. I'm under a lot of stress*, I thought. *I'm in middle school.*

She added, "Whatever this is it will probably go away. Just try to relax."

Probably!?!

"I'm going to prescribe a cream for you to put on the"—she paused—"affected area."

"You mean my entire body?" I said.

"Yes," she answered, typing away on her laptop.

My mom seemed relieved. She had complete faith in doctors, like they were the smartest people on the planet who never made mistakes. If a doctor was telling her that her orange daughter was perfectly fine, that a little cream would make everything better, who was she to argue?

When we got home, Fej saw me for the first time that day.

"Whoa! That's awesome! How did you do that?" He reached over and touched my cheek.

"Quit it," I said, swatting him away.

"The doctor said it will probably just go away." My mom was trying to sound like everything was absolutely fine. "She just needs a special cream."

"PROBABLY?!" shouted Fej. It was the best thing that had happened in his life in a long, long time and he couldn't stop smiling.

My dad, hearing all the shouting, came in to see what was going on. He'd gone to work by the time I woke up that morning. This was the first time he'd seen me since I'd become the color of a Cheeto. He took one look at me and turned to my mother for an explanation.

"The doctor said it'll probably just go away," she said, repeating her mantra like she was in some sort of trance.

My dad looked back at me, standing there in the kitchen like a human Popsicle. "Probably?" he said. Fej laughed.

"Well, on the plus side, I hear boys really like the color orange," Fej said with a smirk.

I squinted at him, furious.

"Are you serious? That is so mean! This is not funny!" I yelled. I stomped up to my room to apply medicated lotion to my entire body.

It smelled like bacon that was cooked in mouthwash and I had to breathe through my mouth.

I texted Lotti.

Hey.

Hey. Where were you today?

At the doctor.

Can you FaceTime?

Promise me you won't freak out

Um . . . ?????????

TWENTY

My phone rang and I saw Lotti's face. But, more important, she saw mine.

"Greta! *Oh* my god, what happened? Did you fall asleep in a tanning bed?" She was laughing a little, but it didn't hurt. Hearing the lightness in her voice and just seeing her face made me smile for the first time since I'd woken up.

I told her about the special cream and how the doctor said the orange would probably go away.

"Does it feel weird?" Lotti asked, scrunching up her nose. I described my skin peeling off my body like a rubber suit and she clapped her hand over her mouth.

"It didn't hurt at all," I assured her.

"It was kind of like when you get sunburned and you start to peel, except it was . . . thick . . . and everywhere." I hadn't told my mom or Dr. Saluja about the shedding, it seemed too dramatic, something that would make my mom flip out even more than she already had.

After a few seconds, Lotti shrugged. "Honestly?" she said. "Compared to spontaneous boobs and period stuff? It's not that weird. It's kind of beautiful, don't you think?"

I loved Lotti.

TWENTY-ONE

Despite my desperate pleas, my mom drove me to school the next day armed with a note that just said: *Please excuse my daughter's orange skin. It is a medical condition and will probably go away.* I wore a black long-sleeved shirt and jeans trying to cover as much of my body as possible. I let my wild curls spring unleashed, hoping that they would act as a distraction. I considered wearing gloves to cover up my hands but decided against it.

"You'll have to take the bus home, sweetie, I have to go over some stuff with the realtor at the new house," she said, looking at me with concern. "It'll be okay. I really do think the cream is working already!" Her forced smile as she reached out to touch my cheek made me want to scream.

"Great," I said. I got out of the car like I was jumping into icy water, holding my breath.

My motto of *Above all, do not call attention to yourself* now seemed like a terrible joke. The whole school was full of eyes following me down the hall. I lost track of the number of *Oh my god*s and *Nice tan, idiot*s that echoed around me as I passed by.

I was trying to disappear into a chair in Mr. Lee's class when Sydney Coorly sat down at the desk right next to me. Needless to say, no one else wanted to sit there. She gave me a quick glance, but not at my skin. She looked me in the eyes. It was the first time anyone but Lotti had done that all day. It must have been a relief to her to have me there. After all, who cares about big boobs when there's an Oompa Loompa in the school?

There are about a thousand kids in the middle school and by the end of fourth period it felt like almost every single one of them had made some sarcastic comment, did a double take, or straight-up laughed in my face. Two days ago, just one person laughing at me would have been devastating. But after it happens to you for several hours straight? Let's just say it's amazing what you can get used to. It's like if you say a completely normal word like . . . oh, I don't know, *pumpkin* or *spray tan* or *freak*, over and over again it starts to sound like nonsense, like you're speaking a foreign language.

Because the principal's office had spread the word to all my teachers that I had a medical condition, none of them mentioned my strange color. And since they were pretending everything was normal for forty-two minutes at a time, I mostly got a break from the obnoxious comments and just had to deal with the looks of disgust on people's faces. It was like they were being forced to sit in a classroom with a piece of roadkill plopped on one of the desks.

When the bell rang, and everyone stood up gathering their stuff, someone would inevitably call me a freak through a fake cough. *Wow*, I thought, *how original*.

Lotti's detailed stories at lunch about the idiotic (well, she used the word *cute*) things that Evan did in class were a welcome distraction.

"He's so funny. We were working on simplifying equations in algebra, and he was like, 'It would be even *simpler* if we just didn't have to do it.'" Lotti laughed like he was a comic genius. I tried to laugh, too, but it wasn't easy.

"I don't know, I think he still likes me?" she went on. "It's kinda hard to tell." She shrugged as she shoveled mac and cheese (that I couldn't help but notice was very close to the color of my new skin) into her mouth. I had to look away.

Over Lotti's shoulder, I saw Derek walking toward our table. I stared down at my tray. My whole body tightened.

He sneered at me, "What a surprise, you ended up being

a total freak who only wants to hang out with girls." He barely looked at me when he said this. But just that one sentence, that one angry glance in my direction made me feel like I'd been slapped.

"Keep walking, dipstick...," said Lotti through a mouthful of food. I'm sure he didn't even hear her, but I did, and I gave her a little smile. My skin made him not even want to look at me. I felt like I was wearing a shield.

Lotti rolled her eyes "What a tool. Do you want me to ask Evan to say something to him?"

"What? God, no! I just want to forget that Derek even exists." I pushed my tray out in front of me and sat back in my chair. I'd suddenly lost my appetite.

Getting through the day was not enough. It was time to take the bus home. The lawlessness of the school bus was terrifying on a normal day, so it felt like there were weights in my shoes as I climbed up the stairs. The bus driver, Mrs. Flax, looked at me and shook her head like I was a juvenile delinquent. Like I had dyed my entire body bright orange just to ruin her day.

Kids I didn't even know were shouting at me as I walked down the aisle.

"Nice tan, Goodwin!"

"Orange you glad you're not Greta!"

"Halloween isn't for another month, dork!"

"Greta, are you orange? Or is it just a *pigment* of my imagination!" This last one was from Sean Dolittle. He was a dorky kid who usually got the brunt of this stuff, so he was thrilled to be on the other side for once. Of course his joke was a little too sophisticated for this crowd and he didn't get the reaction he thought he would. He sat back down and tried to be invisible again.

I found a seat by a window and pressed my forehead against the cold glass. Luckily my stop was only a few minutes away.

***

The first thing I heard when I walked in the door to my house was the jangly sound of glass being swept up from the floor. My mom rearranged her face when she saw me.

"One less glass I have to pack," she said, trying to be cheerful. "How was school?" she asked me in mid-sweep.

"It went pretty much like you would expect," I mumbled as I dropped my backpack and opened the fridge, careful not to step on the little pile of glass.

"I'm sure it'll get better," she said.

"Well that makes one of us," I said, stuffing a rubbery rectangle of cheese in my mouth.

"Remember the time your dad fell asleep at the beach and turned bright red, like a lobster? I ended up having to take him to the ER and I missed Aunt Katie's wedding," she said, clearly remembering how annoyed she'd been.

"I remember," I said. "This is totally different." I turned and stomped up to my room.

TWENTY-TWO

That weekend we all had to go to Fej's baseball game. I guess turning bright orange is no excuse not to support your little brother. His team is called the Hornets, and they're terrible.

I sat with my parents, hiding under my gray hoodie. Fej was an outfielder, and not only did he not care that we were there to cheer him on, but he didn't even seem to notice that he was in the middle of an actual baseball game. He was pretending to slide into home plate, using his glove (which was supposed to be on his hand) as the base. Then he'd stand up and cheer like he was the star of his imaginary game. I couldn't really blame him. Poor guy was bored out of his mind. Their pitcher was so bad that he walked every single batter. There was no way anyone was gonna hit a ball. But my dad kept shouting, "Look alive out there, Jeffrey!" and clapping, trying to get his attention. I don't know why he cared so much. They were third graders.

I texted Lotti to pass the time.

                                                   Hey

Hey

                    SO very happy to spend my Saturday at a baseball game where no one knows how to play. My brother is really rocking it. He's currently talking to himself in left field

Oh my god. At least you don't have sisters.
Angie just yelled at me for using her green nail polish, like it's the end of the freakin' world.

                    People are the worst
Maybe you should start taking everything out of her room when she's at school and burying it in the backyard

OMG you're a genius
But I might have to come live with you.

She would literally make my life hell

                                This idea's getting better all the time!

LOL

My mom tapped me on the shoulder.

"Want to go get a snack?" she asked, handing me a five-dollar bill. It was currently the eighth inning. The bases were loaded because the pitcher had thrown every ball into the dirt or way above the batters' heads and the score was . . . zero to zero.

I sighed. "Yeah, okay."

My dad handed me another five. "Grab a snack for your old dad, huh? Something really terrible for me." He winked at my mom, and she teasingly punched him in the arm.

There was a snack table full of homemade cookies, brownies, and cupcakes. I smiled as I walked up to Mrs. *Somebody*. I could never remember her name, but she was always at these games. Apparently it was her calling in life to provide snacks and unearned enthusiasm for eight-year-old boys pretending to play baseball.

"Hi Greta. Wow, you've got quite a suntan!" she said.

I sighed. "Yup," I said. As I tried to decide what to get, I heard some boys talking behind me.

"Hey, it's the freak from school. Derek, didn't you make out with her at Greg's party?" One of them snorted. He sounded like a mouth breather.

My whole body tightened. I had no idea why Derek would be at this stupid game, but I felt like the sky suddenly went silvery bright and the ground beneath me was spinning. I froze.

"No way, man, are you kidding? That's gross. I don't even know that girl."

I felt like I was going to throw up.

I forced my feet to move and turned and walked away.

My brain was spinning with the memory of Derek's wet, gummy mouth pushing against my face. His greedy hands grabbing at me relentlessly. Hearing Derek say that he'd never touched me, that he didn't even know who I was—*I don't even know that girl*, he'd said—made me feel like I was in a nightmare. Somehow the comment he'd snarled at me in the cafeteria, the angry look on his face, those were nothing compared to this. The fact that he denied even knowing me, that he acted like I was just some freak in school that he'd never even met, this was worse. Much worse. I hated him.

I finally got back to where my parents were sitting in the bleachers.

"Where's my processed sugar and high-fructose corn

syrup?" asked my dad. I handed the money back to my mom.

"They were all sold out," I said. My mom reached her arm around my shoulders and pulled me toward her.

I felt her eyes through the side of my hoodie. She knew something was wrong. But she also knew better than to ask me about it right then.

TWENTY-THREE

I don't like to admit that my mom is *ever* right, but *Did you see Greta Goodwin? She's orange!* became old news faster than I thought it would. It was only a week before someone had tripped holding a tray of spaghetti, a girl walked around with a period stain on her pants the whole first half of the day without realizing it, and one of the teachers actually farted in front of his whole class.

It was the one thing that saved me. Middle schoolers have a very short attention span.

By the end of that week the boys especially went back to being oblivious to the fact that I even existed. Turns out, big boobs are never boring and poor Sydney Coorly was back under the spotlight. I was walking behind her in the hallway, and here I was, a girl with bright orange skin, and I was still invisible compared to Sydney. Boys openly stared at her as she walked by, as if her body was an invitation.

The reaction from girls was just as bad. I saw sneers and eye rolls, half-hearted attempts at hiding a laugh. Sydney had done nothing to them but somehow, they had gotten it in their heads that her body was a betrayal. It was clear as I walked behind her hunched shoulders that nobody felt that more than she did. *I'm lucky*, I thought. *This orange skin may be weird, but it's mine. No one wants to take it from me.*

At home, even my mom stopped looking at me through a rigid smile as she tried to hide the panic in her eyes. She seemed to have convinced herself that the lotion was actually working.

"Ya know, the orange has really faded! Your color looks much better!" she'd say in a chipper voice when I came down for breakfast.

My poor mother was delusional.

Dr. Saluja's assurance that this would "probably go away" was not coming true and she had to face facts. I could almost hear her thoughts: *It's fine. It's perfectly fine. My daughter is orange and it's totally fine.*

Before *the shedding*, when I looked in the mirror I used to focus on things like my frizzy hair and chubby cheeks. I would study how my nose was too wide, my eyes not the almond shape that was a true mark of beauty. I used to sit there and make a mental list of all the ways that I fell short of being beautiful. But lately, I didn't even notice those things. I studied my reflection like I was staring into a sunset, the color radiating back at me.

But, as crazy as it sounds, I was starting to like my new skin.

The brightness of the orange gave me an untouchable glow. I'd seen cartoon characters with skin my color. Like everything in a cartoon, the colors were high energy, vibrant versions of reality. But when you watched the show, you didn't even notice it because nothing was real anyway. Sometimes my actual life felt like that to me, so it was starting to make some sense.

My haircut was now the least ridiculous thing about me, and I stopped trying to tame it into something acceptable. I let it shout at people, my curls reaching out from my head as I passed by: *Yeah, I'm orange and I might be crazy, so what?*

I had always known that although weird stuff was definitely going to go on with my thirteen-year-old body, there were rules about what could *actually* happen.

Now I knew that wasn't true.

All bets were off as far as what was coming next.

I looked in the mirror at my bizarre reflection, my skin the color of a perfectly ripe peach. I had always thought that there was only one way to be beautiful, one way to change.

Turns out I was wrong.

TWENTY-FOUR

I was getting something out of my locker when a girl with purple hair came up to me. She was in my art class, and it seemed like she changed her hair color every few days. We'd never really talked.

"I think your skin is awesome," she said. She seemed to think I'd done this to myself on purpose, like I'd been soaking in a bath of Gatorade every night, trying to get the perfect shade of orange.

"Thanks," I said. "I like your hair this color."

She smiled and pulled a strand of lavender in front of her eyes like she had to remember which color it was.

"I'm Astrid," she said.

"I'm Greta."

"Yeah, I know. Your name was all over school. People are

idiots. Did you know your name means 'pearl'? It's German," she said.

I snorted a laugh. "Nope, I had no idea."

"How long is that gonna last?" she said, pointing at my face.

"I have no idea," I said again.

"Cool." She nodded. "See ya around." She gracefully stepped into the crowded hallway and disappeared like a salmon swimming upstream.

Art was one of the few classes that Lotti and I had together, and later that day we were doing something called "blind contour drawing." We had to pair up and draw pictures of our partners without looking at the paper, just staring at each other's faces. I was concentrating hard on the feathery curve of Lotti's eyebrow when Astrid walked by us and said, "Hey."

Lotti looked at me like I had been keeping a secret from her.

"You know that girl?" Her pencil never left her page as she stared at the back of Astrid's purple head. Her drawing was just going to look like a bunch of scribbles, but Ms. Crick would praise it like it belonged in a museum. Ms. Crick loved Lotti.

"Yeah, her name's Astrid. She's cool," I said. I went back to staring at Lotti's eye like I was in a trance.

I kept sneaking looks down at my drawing. The spot on

the paper where Lotti's eye should have been looked like I'd squashed a bug on the page. It was hard to believe I had been concentrating so hard. It looked like a toddler had done it. Or maybe a monkey. You know what? I've seen drawings on the internet done by monkeys, theirs were better.

Ms. Crick was walking around the classroom, looking at everyone's ridiculous squiggle drawings, praising random ones for their "line quality" and "expressiveness." Of course one of the ones she chose was Lotti's. "You've really captured her essence. Great job, Lotti," she said, patting her shoulder. I peeked down at her drawing. Like I suspected, it looked like she had dropped a wad of black string on her page.

"It's like looking in a mirror, Lotti!" I said.

She snorted.

Lotti was in a different section of gym than me this year, so I was usually pretty stressed during the whole forty minutes, wondering if I was sweating more than other people. Without Lotti there, there was no one to ask.

We were doing a section on volleyball, which as far as I was concerned was just a slightly more civilized form of dodgeball. I would stand there with my hands clasped in front of me, arms straight, looking like I was begging for mercy as some girl on the other side of the net would launch a speeding ball at me. Ignoring the human impulse to duck or run I would close my eyes and try to stop this bullet with the soft underbelly of my wrists. I wasn't great at it. Like almost everything I did, I was fine.

A girl I didn't know with a high bouncy ponytail was serving for the other team. Her innocent smile turned into a pinched, angry face of determination, like she was suddenly possessed by a volleyball demon, right before she punched the ball. She made a loud grunting noise that sounded like it came from someone twice her size, like she was picturing someone's face when she hit it. Someone she hated. It was like a meteor shooting over the net. The ball went directly between me and another girl. We both yelled.

"Mine!" And I dove for it.

When I stretched my arms and back to get the ball, which would have normally been just out of reach, I could feel my muscles working in a rhythm, fluidly guiding me to exactly where I needed to be. It was as if my skin was expanding, allowing everything that my body was capable of to happen. I felt the ripple of my muscles moving up through my spine toward the ball like a wave. The ball landed perfectly on my outstretched wrist and arched back over the net.

"Good get, Greta!" yelled Mrs. Richards, clapping her hands. My cheeks warmed with pride, and I stood a little taller. My new skin was not just a different color, it allowed my whole body to move differently. I was graceful. The girl next to me gave me a quick nod. "Nice," she said.

Later at lunch, the cafeteria was so loud that Lotti and I finally grabbed our trays and went to the bathroom to finish eating in there.

"Ah, now this is more like it!" I said, sliding down the wall. I raised my pinkie as I took a long sip of my chocolate milk. "Classy," I added, my voice echoey in the little tiled room. Lotti laughed. Suddenly someone flushed a toilet. A makeup girl looked down at us like we were cockroaches. We sat staring at the pipes twisting like snakes under the row of sinks, waiting for her to leave.

As she did, Astrid came in and walked confidently over to where we were sitting on the floor. Her hair was the color of a tropical ocean this week. She sat down right next to Lotti.

"Hey," she said. Lotti's face was nervous, but I saw the tension ease from her mouth when Astrid, seemingly a girl of very few words, just said, "I like the drawing you did of Greta. You're a really good artist."

"Yeah, she's so good, she doesn't even need to use her eyes!" I said, leaning into Lotti's shoulder a little.

Lotti blushed and gave us a smirky smile. "Your hair looks really cool this color," she told Astrid.

"Thanks," Astrid said, absently tugging at the ends. "One of these days it's just gonna fall out, I keep dyeing it so much. Then I'll *really* be popular!"

All three of us laughed and the sound bounced around the tiles like music.

"Okay, see you in art," she said, getting up. She took a quick look at herself in one of the mirrors above the sink, smiled a little, and turned and waved goodbye.

"She's awesome," said Lotti.

"I know, right?" I said.

"Wanna come over this weekend?" she asked.

"You know I do."

TWENTY-FIVE

I was braiding Lotti's hair as we sat on her bed. It was soft and felt cool on my fingers as I expertly moved the silky strands into place. I loved playing with her hair. She was talking about Evan again.

"We're gonna go to the Sweet Tooth after school on Monday."

The Sweet Tooth was a frozen yogurt place where you could put on your own toppings. They had everything from candy to actual fruit. People tended to bunch up at the crushed-candy selection. There was never anyone over by the fruit. The only problem was that you didn't realize until they weighed the thing at checkout that your little cup could hold five pounds' worth of M&M's, cookie crumbles, and Jolly Rancher Bites. It would end up costing way more than you thought it would and you couldn't exactly put it back.

Somehow I never learned this lesson and every time I went there, I piled on toppings like it was my last meal.

"Wow! That's, like, a date!" I said to the top of Lotti's head. "Maybe you should skip the gummy worms this time, though."

She reached behind her and slapped at my butt. Her braces were like gummy-worm traps and although it was a great source of entertainment for us, it probably wasn't something she'd want to show Evan.

These days most of Lotti's interests revolved around him and, I would never tell her this, but it was kind of boring. I hadn't told her that much about the night of Greg's party, I didn't want to think about it. There wasn't really any point. Derek was completely ignoring me now and I no longer had to hold my breath around every corner, afraid that he'd jump out at me. That his face would suddenly be as close as it was that night, that my body would be within reach of his tentacle-like hands.

My new skin had formed like a shell around me. It separated me from the world just enough that I didn't disappear into it like I usually did. It used to be that my skin was just a flimsy bit of fabric stretched over my body like I was a piece of furniture. Delicate fabric that could easily be poked or punctured and bruised. The orange skin was like a giant muscle, protecting my body. I thought about the pictures that Mr. Lee had shown us of the insects. Their skeletons on the outside of their bodies. It made sense to me. Why have the strongest part of your body, your bones, be deep inside? This new skin of mine felt protective and proud and although it wasn't hard like bones, I felt safe underneath. Now when boys looked at me, or *didn't* look at me, I felt powerful. I wasn't just a collection of body parts waiting for inspection. I was something completely different. And even if that also meant I was completely freaky? It still somehow felt better.

As Lotti went on about every little thing the doofus did at school, I noticed her dark chocolaty hair wound around my peach-colored fingers. It was beautiful. The sound of Lotti's voice was like soft music, drifting around the room. I know it sounds strange, considering the fact that I was now the biggest freak in the school, but I couldn't remember ever being this happy.

TWENTY-SIX

When I saw Lotti waiting for me by the front doors of school Monday morning everything had changed. Not for me this time, but for Lotti. She was wearing a smile like a mask. Something was wrong.

"What happened?" I asked her. The smile disappeared and she started to cry.

"Greta, people are saying stuff about me." Her breath was catching in her throat as she tried to talk.

"What do you mean?" I asked. She looked down and it was a couple of seconds before she could bring her face back up to meet my eyes.

"People are calling me a slut." Her face crumbled and she started to shake with tears.

"What? What are you talking about?" It had only been a matter of hours. But that's how it works in middle school.

Everything happens in hyperdrive. We started heading toward her locker.

"I don't get it," she said, her eyes wide with fear as they scanned the faces around us. "They're saying that I did stuff with Evan that I didn't do. We just made out."

As Lotti and I walked down the hallway, the whispering of kids who were giddy with the tingle of gossip surrounded us like smoke. I was used to these cold stares by now, but Lotti wasn't. I could feel her body tense up next to me. I looped her arm in mine, wanting to protect her. It seemed like every other boy that walked past her gave her a predatory smile or said something like, "Hey Lotti," like they were in on a secret together. Each time she heard it, she flinched.

The girls were just as bad, looking at my best friend, who was shrinking beside me, as if she was strutting down the hall in stilettos and a bikini. They would sneer something to the girl next to them and start typing frantically on their phones. I stuck my tongue out at them and glared. I felt anger, like electricity, pulsing through my blood and I wanted to take them all on.

We stood next to each other at her locker. I was trying to give her a pep talk that would last until I saw her again at lunch.

"Lotti, they're such idiots. Besides, if they can stop concentrating on the fact that I have orange skin, they'll forget this stupid rumor, too. You'll see." She nodded, but her eyes were blank. I could tell that it was taking everything she had not to turn and run out of the school.

"You can do this," I said. I squeezed her arm and bonked her on the nose. I felt the muscles in my body ripple down through my fingers and strengthen Lotti, just a little bit.

The lunchroom was buzzing. Unlike with my skin change, when kids would back away from me slightly while they were calling me names, people were walking right by our table and even in the deafening noise of the cafeteria we could hear them whisper, "Slut."

That's it, I thought. I stood up tall and rigid, my muscles thundering beneath my skin as I leaned toward them. "Get AWAY from her!" I growled, my voice strong and menacing. "You don't know anything about her, you bunch of feeble-minded doorknobs! You're all slack-jawed, parasitic duck bags! She's a freaking queen! And you all are just a mob of boob-hungry, mouth-breathing, knuckle-dragging, clueless, dirt-nozzled turkey stains!"

A teacher was coming toward me. I knew I was gonna be in huge trouble, but I couldn't stop. My anger was like a junkyard dog they'd been poking with a stick, and I was finally letting it off the chain. "You're all a bunch of hypocrites! All you think about is who you want to slobber your penis breath all over, you mediocre, potato-headed, Barbie-brained sex maniacs! You're all just a bunch of toe-slurping NOOBS!"

By now, the lunch monitor was two feet away. I could tell she was afraid to touch my orange skin, which by now was vibrating with anger.

But I had to be stopped.

"This is totally unacceptable, Greta Goodwin. Let's go." She had hold of my elbow through my shirt and was dragging me away from the crowd.

"What's *unacceptable* is the fact that you're all dim-witted, drooling puberty monkeys with nothing better to do than make up stuff about the only person in this school whose trash is worth more than all you stupid stink lizards put together!"

We were on our way to the principal's office and as I looked over my shoulder, I saw Lotti standing perfectly still, her hands clasped over her mouth.

Adrenaline was still pumping through my body like lava while the principal, Mr. Gordon, explained to me that angry name-calling like that had no place in our school. I had to pinch my mouth shut hard so I wouldn't argue that what those kids were saying was much, much worse than anything I had said. They were all probably laughing about what I'd done by now. But Lotti was never going to laugh at what they were calling her. "I'm contacting your mother. You will be suspended for the rest of the day. This is not like you, Greta. I'm very disappointed."

I sat on the cold wooden bench outside his office while I waited for my mom to pick me up.

When I got in the car my mom just shook her head. "We'll talk about this when we get home. I have a million things I have to do today and picking you up from the principal's office was *not* one of them." She gave me a quick angry glance. "We have to stop and get some more boxes." Anything that had to do with the move was top priority and for once I was glad.

I leaned against the window, watching the road behind us through the side mirror, unrolling like a spool of black thread. It was like looking at the past and it made me feel something like hunger, but through my whole body, not just my stomach.

"How many more boxes do you think you'll need for your room, Greta?" she asked me.

Considering I still had the three she had given me over a month ago, stacked up in a corner, it was hard to say. I knew that if I didn't come up with something, though, my mom would not be pleased, and we'd suddenly be in an argument that I was sick of having.

"Two more should be good," I said.

An hour later we walked into the house and my mom changed gears completely.

"Now, are you going to tell me what happened today? Having an angry tirade in the school cafeteria? Calling people names? Being sent *home*! This is *not* the Greta I know."

I wanted to say that she was right. I was *not* the Greta she knew. I was not the girl who thought the best thing to do when I was furious, when I just couldn't take being made to feel afraid all the time, when my best friend in the world, who I loved more than anything, was being attacked, was to pretend. To smile. God forbid I was an angry girl; there's even a word for girls who show their anger. And no one wanted to be called one of those. As far as I knew, there was no such word to describe an angry boy. He was just mad.

"Mom," I pleaded with her. "You don't understand. They were being so mean to Lotti. They were calling her a horrible name." My mom raised her eyebrows in the middle, just a little bit. She let me keep going.

"Some kids started a rumor about her that's *not* true. I had to say something!"

"What exactly *did* you say?" she asked me, her arms crossed in front of her chest, bracing herself for whatever was coming.

"I said they were a bunch of boob-obsessed, mouth-breathing puberty monkeys. And that they were hypocrites."

I could tell my mom was concentrating on keeping a

serious face. I was still in trouble, but it was kind of funny. She closed her eyes and shook her head, trying to pull it together.

"Okay," she finally said. "Just go to your room. I need to talk to your father. This is not behavior that we expect from you, Greta."

"Fine," I said. I couldn't wait to get to my room.

I got a text from Lotti.

You ok?

> **Yeah.**
>
> **Still waiting to hear how long**
>
> **I'll be imprisoned for my crimes**

You were awesome today.

Thanks (bonk)

> **I unleashed the hounds! Lol**
>
> **Totally worth it (bonk)**

I was starting to fall asleep waiting for my mom to come tell me how deeply disappointed in me she was when I heard her fingernails on my door.

"Come in," I said, sitting upright.

My mom sat down next to me and let out a long breath.

"What happened today was unacceptable." Ugh. That word again.

She paused.

"It sounds like there's some pretty difficult stuff going on for Lotti. I respect the fact that you wanted to protect her, I do. But screaming and calling people names is not okay. I don't know what your classmates were saying about her, but I do know how mean kids can be. How hard it is to be in middle school."

She had a look on her face that seemed far away. Like she was remembering something that she didn't want to think about. "Poor Lotti," she said.

"Mom, she's really sad right now. She needs me. Do you think I could go over to her house and make sure she's okay? I mean, the 'grounding me until I'm twenty' or the 'hard labor' or whatever it is that you're gonna do to punish me, can it wait until after I go see her?"

We looked at each other in silence for a second, and she smiled. She wrapped her pinkie around mine. "Okay. But we might ground you until you're twenty-one," she said.

TWENTY-SEVEN

When I got to Lotti's room that night, she was curled up on her bed, holding Winky, the one-eyed stuffed rabbit that she'd had since she was a baby. Its ears were bent, and worn on the spots where she used to rub them against her lips, to soothe herself to sleep.

I crawled in next to her.

I spooned her and hugged her tight.

"Why would they say that?" Her question hung in the room, mixing with the dust particles that floated in the musty air, which felt damp from all the crying and nose blowing.

"I don't know," I said, "because they're boring idiots who have nothing else to do?"

She turned and looked at me for the first time.

"I have no idea," I said. "I think it's like a lot of things, it just . . . happened." We both looked at my orange hand resting on my hip.

I hugged her and we lay there in silence for a long time.

"Dinner," Lotti's mom called from downstairs. Mrs. Messina was an amazing cook, and I felt my mouth start to water at the thought of what might be waiting for us.

"I'm starving," I said. Lotti gave me a little smile and we went downstairs.

The Messinas made a big deal out of all their meals, unlike at home, where we seemed to have to cater to Fej's strict diet of noodles and cheese with some vegetables haunting the side of the plate, just begging to be eaten before they got stone cold.

Mrs. Messina plopped a huge portion of lasagna on my plate. It was glorious. The steam rose like dry ice onstage at a concert, and I had to stop myself from letting out a *Wooo!* and punching my fist in the air. She could see my excitement, and nothing made Mrs. Messina happier.

"Eat!" she said, smiling. "There's plenty more!" Lotti and I exchanged looks. She was rolling her eyes, I was licking my lips.

Lotti had four brothers and sisters. There were eight of us

and more food was being passed along the perimeter of the table like it was on a conveyor belt. As usual, some sort of 1980s retro music was blaring from a speaker in the kitchen, Lotti's mom dancing a little in her chair as she ate, occasionally using her fork like a microphone, her dad smiling and humming along. The whole family was talking at the same time. It was a much different kind of chaos from what went on at the cafeteria at school. This house was full of love. And it tasted delicious.

When I came back to my house after being at Lotti's, it always seemed so quiet. Tonight my mom and dad were waiting for me in the kitchen. Dad was cleaning up after their noodle dinner, scraping sad broccoli into the sink. "Your mom tells me you took on the world today," he said. He gave me a quick look while he was sudsing the plates.

Mom was sitting at the table. "How's Lotti?" she asked.

I looked back and forth between them. "Not great. I'm sorry I got in trouble," I said. "I won't do it again."

"It's late," she said. "We'll talk about it tomorrow." She gave me a half smile.

"You know, I think that cream is really working. The orange is fading a bit, don't ya think?"

I looked down at my hands, turning them over and over. And the first thought that came into my head surprised me: *Oh! I hope not, I don't want to go back!*

"Maybe," I said.

"Good night, my little hooligan," she said, looking at me with hopeful eyes.

When I got to my bed, I fell asleep almost instantly with just the sound of crickets outside my window.

TWENTY-EIGHT

It happened again.

I woke up after a restless night of wriggling and pulling at my skin. This time a huge piece had gotten caught on my right thigh as I tried to push it off. I yanked at the orange flap, which felt like vinyl. It was thicker this time, and the effort was exhausting. My fingers ached. I stretched it as hard as I could, feeling it slowly unpeel from my body. The new skin underneath felt powdery and smooth compared to the sticky pile mingling with my feet at the bottom of the bed. I slowly brought my hand out from under the covers. It looked like green sea glass. I held it in front of my face, turning it like I was looking at some sort of precious jewel. It was slightly translucent. My skin had turned the color of mint chocolate chip ice cream. There were traces of the orange shining like gold veins. *Well*, I thought. *It could be worse. I could be beige.* I hated the color beige.

When I walked into the kitchen, Fej spit his orange juice all over his cereal.

"Whoa! Cool! You look like a shamrock shake! Hey Mom, can I get one of those?" Drops of juice dribbled down his chin.

My mom turned around from the coffee maker and spilled her fresh cup all over the front of her shirt.

"Greta! What happened?" She couldn't help herself. She knew that I didn't have the foggiest idea what had happened. I shrugged and sat down at the table. My dad looked at me like he was studying a painting, speechless.

"I'm calling Dr. Saluja," Mom said, wiping the front of her coffee-stained shirt.

This time Dr. Saluja literally froze when she opened the door and saw me sitting on the paper sheet, like a big stick of peppermint gum. My mom's face was pleading with her, *Please tell us this is normal, please tell us this is normal* . . . Dr. Saluja seemed nervous to touch me as she examined my skin.

"How do you feel?" she asked, trying to keep the panic out of her voice.

"Fine," I said. And I did. I honestly felt better than fine. There was a tiny glow underneath my skin that felt like something a yoga teacher would talk about.

Your inner beauty . . .
Follow your inner light . . .
Your light within . . .

I didn't look radioactive or anything. It was barely visible, this light. But people could see it if they looked closely.

Dr. Saluja did her usual tests, listening to my heart, telling me to take several deep breaths while she put the cold metal of the stethoscope on my back. It made my skin ripple slightly, like my body was one of those massage chairs.

I think she was just trying to buy herself some time, because she kept saying, ". . . and again . . . and again."

I thought I was going to pass out from all that heavy breathing.

"Okay," she said, letting out a deep breath of her own as she turned to my mom.

"I think that whatever this is, it's an improvement on the orange. Her vitals sound perfect. Her heart is strong, her lungs sound good. We could do more tests, or we could see where this goes. Give it a little time. For now, I'd like to refer you to a dermatologist." She typed away into her laptop, grateful to be handing this insanity over to someone else.

I did not want to be stuck with more needles.

"I feel really good," I said, looking hopefully at my mom. Dr. Saluja gave us a pretend smile as she snapped her laptop closed.

"Good luck," she said. "I'm sure Dr. Conti will have a better idea about what kind of treatment will be best." She looked at my mom, careful not to make eye contact with me, and turned and left, shutting the door hard behind her. Obviously, she could not leave that room fast enough.

When I got home, I got a text from Lotti.

Where were you today???

> It happened again.
> Wait til you see what color I am . . .

**FaceTime!
Now!** ☺

When I popped up on Lotti's screen, she gasped. "Greta, you're the color of sea glass! I love sea glass!" Her hands were pressed together in front of her mouth, her eyes wide with joyful surprise.

"You're like a piece from my collection!" she squealed. Only Lotti could make me feel like something precious and rare and not freakish and gross.

Our phones illuminated our smiles as we held each other's faces in our hands.

"Ta-da," I said.

TWENTY-NINE

The waiting room at the dermatologist was very different from Dr. Saluja's office. There was music playing that was supposed to make us think we were deep in a forest, but with someone standing next to us playing the flute . . . veerrryyy slowly. All the furniture was rounded and covered in white leather-ish material. There were pamphlets fanned out on all the tables. Each one had a picture of a beautiful woman smiling dreamily under ads for Botox and skin peels. I picked up one that had an ad for some kind of concoction that *provides defense against environmental stressors. Okay,* I thought. *I might put that one all over my body . . .*

I'm not sure exactly what a skin peel is, but if people are signing up to get this done on purpose? It does make what keeps happening to me feel less bizarre. Although none of the women in these pictures are green.

"Greta," said a woman with long mahogany hair. She was dressed in blue scrubs, which I guess were supposed to make her seem professional. But she looked more like an actress playing the part of a nurse. Her face seemed to have been airbrushed on by a team of makeup artists.

As she led us to an exam room, she didn't mention anything about my skin. This woman was *not* going to break character.

"Okay, Greta, take everything off except your underwear and put on the gown with the opening in the back. Dr. Conti will be in shortly." Her gleaming smile never left her face and she turned and left the room.

I was waiting for a director somewhere to yell, *CUT. That was great, Savannah. Let's do it again but this time try to look a little more . . . human.*

When Dr. Conti came in, she was just as perfectly put together, but her smile drooped a little when she saw me sitting on the chair. I must've looked like I made my skin this color on purpose so I wouldn't clash with the turquoise paper gown. I don't know what she was expecting, but it was not this.

As she composed herself, it was almost visible, the mask of "health-care professional" falling back over her face like a veil.

"I'm Dr. Conti. Can you tell me a little about what's going on, Greta?" She tilted her head like I had been keeping this whole thing a secret, but it was okay, it was time to tell the truth.

"I have no idea," I said.

She asked the same questions that Dr. Saluja had asked. "Any new creams, lotions, soaps? Change in diet?"

My mom told her about the medicated stuff that I'd been slathering over my whole body.

"Okay. Well, let's stop using the cream for now." She snapped on a pair of blue gloves and rolled her stool up very close to my face, shining a little bright light on my cheek. I felt her rubber finger barely touching me, as if I might suddenly bite.

After a few seconds of silence, she asked me, "How do you feel, Greta?" This time she was looking directly into my eyes. Her face was open, like she was genuinely curious.

"Actually, I feel amazing," I said.

"Really? How so?" she asked.

"I don't know, it's hard to explain. I feel really . . . beautiful, and strong. Kind of like a light was turned on inside of me."

Her rubber-gloved hand touched my forehead. "Have you been having fevers?"

I realized I wasn't explaining this very well. How could I tell this woman that being under this new skin made me feel more alive? I was no longer exposed to every single criticism or comparison that might come at me. Who's gonna comment on how flat chested I am, how weird my haircut is, or if I'm a few pounds heavier? I'm freakin' *green* for god's sake! I was something different now. For the first time since I was little, my body was something I felt good in; I wasn't wishing it was different.

But I just shrugged. "No. No fevers," I said.

She pushed back on her wheely stool, retreating to her laptop.

She said she was going to prescribe another cream. Hopefully this one would smell better.

When we got back in the car, my mom was still putting on her seat belt as I turned to face her.

"I don't want to do this anymore," I said.

"Greta, what are you . . . ?"

"Mom." I tried to think of a way to explain to her that this was not a problem that she needed to fix. That there was no reason to keep making these appointments. How could I tell my mother that I had never felt comfortable in my old skin? This green was *mine*.

"I don't want to go to any more doctors."

She looked at me, stunned, her mouth slightly open.

"But honey . . . ," she started.

"Mom. Look at me," I said.

She put her hand up, covering her mouth. Her eyes

started to water. For the first time since I started changing, she allowed herself to stare at my face, to really see what I looked like. I held my arm in front of me and lightly stroked the fine, silky hairs that covered my green skin.

I smiled at her. "I'm beautiful," I said. I reached my hand out in front of her face and she held it. She turned it over, softly, watching the color change. The light coming through the windshield warmed my skin so it was the color of a brand-new leaf. She kissed it.

"Yes, Greta," she said, her face softening. "You are."

After a few seconds, she smiled and turned on the car. The hum of the motor signaling the end of the conversation, for now.

THIRTY

The next morning, the hallways at school were full of posters reminding us that the Autumn Dance was coming up. But when everyone saw me, the buzz in the air switched like someone had pushed a button. Walking next to a person with pistachio-colored skin was the break Lotti needed from the spotlight of the rumor that had been following her around. After my rant in the cafeteria, I think people were a little scared to tease me too hard. I was a loose cannon . . . a mint-green cannon.

Today I was armed with a note from my mom for the nurse and anyone else who wanted a useless explanation of my oddity. The note was almost identical to the first one, except this time it said *greenish*. Other than that, it was basically the same experience as last time. I got the muffled fake coughs thinly disguising the word *freak* by every other person who walked by me and the intentional ignorance from the teachers.

Besides the posters, the halls were scattered with construction-paper pumpkins. Every message reminding us to be *respectful* and *responsible* was now surrounded by orange and red paper leaves.

Of course, when everything was turning to fall colors like *orange*, possibly making my skin look like I was just a super big fan of the season . . . my body decided to turn bright green.

THIRTY-ONE

Lotti and I were having a beauty day at my house. We sat on lounge chairs covered in woven plasticky fabric that made a checkerboard pattern on the backs of our thighs. We both had exfoliating masks on our faces, and our skin felt tight and scaly. A tiny part of me wondered if the mint color would come off when I removed the mask, but I figured it was pretty unlikely.

"Actually, this is what it feels like all over my body right before I shed," I said through a mouth that was getting harder to move.

"Really? Cool!" said Lotti, barely moving her lips. "That must be so weird."

I looked out at our backyard. The sandbox that my grandfather built for us was still there. My mom always teased him that it would rust before it fell apart, there were so many nails in it. There was a roof over it to keep it dry. Now it was full of leaves and twigs, and probably all kinds of little critters used it like a litter box. I knew Mom was going to be glad to not have to look at it anymore when we moved to the new house. But even though I would always bang my head into the sharp corner of the roof when I stood up, I was going to miss it. Our yard was small, but I remembered playing dinosaurs here with Lotti and it felt like it was a whole planet.

"So, Evan texted me last night," said Lotti, her lips barely moving under her mask. It had been a while since she'd talked to him. She didn't know if he started the rumor and part of her didn't really want to know.

"Oh my god, really?" My face couldn't move a muscle to make an expression, so I opened my eyes extra wide to show her I was super surprised.

"You know what? He was really sweet. He was checking to see if I was okay. He said that girl who looked like an eighth grader at Greg's party started the rumor. He called her a dizzy-eyed stink minion." She snorted through her shrunken nostrils, I laughed with her.

She had closed her eyes and her head was resting against the slightly prickly lounge chair. "He asked me to go to the Autumn Dance with him." I think she kept her eyes shut so she didn't have to see my reaction right away.

"Are you gonna go?" It was kind of funny having this entire conversation without any expressions, like we were robots imitating humans. It was a bit of a relief to not have to show her an excited face. I had been hoping we'd go together.

"I want to go with *you*," she said. She reached over and grabbed my hand.

I squeezed hers as I said, "Duh, of course you do. I'm a freakin' shamrock shake! Everyone wants some of this!" I pointed my finger up and down my minty body.

Lotti started to laugh. "Don't! You're making my face crack!"

Later that night I was lying in bed admiring the purple nail polish Lotti had put on my fingers. The light coming in my window made my green skin glow like I was an exotic sea creature. I didn't want to sleep. I felt like I needed to get outside.

I lay under my covers for a few minutes, making sure everyone was asleep. Our house was small enough that if someone was awake, I'd hear them. In the new house I probably wouldn't be able to tell if anyone else was even home.

After a couple of minutes of silence, I snuck down the stairs and went out to where Lotti and I had been sitting earlier that day. I walked over to the big tree close to our house. On the trunk it looked like small lacy flowers were blooming out of the bark. We learned about that stuff in science. Was it pronounced *lie-ken* or *lie-chen*? I reached out and touched it. It felt like it was alive and growing beneath my fingers. It was beautiful and strange. Like me.

THIRTY-TWO

In art class we were doing something called exquisite corpse drawings. It sounded pretty ghoulish, and we all looked around the room at one another with slightly frightened faces. We had to get into groups of three.

Astrid walked over to Lotti and me and all three of us smiled with relief.

"Cool color, Greta!" she whispered.

"Thanks," I said.

"Together you're going to create something completely unique that's a combination of all of your creativity! This was something invented by the *surrealist* painters. Surrealists were a group of artists who made paintings that were almost dreamlike. They were very creative, and they did not believe that they had to make art that looked like the real world. This project will unleash your creativity! Now have some fun with it!" Ms. Crick had the enthusiasm of a kindergarten teacher. It tended to make everyone immediately exhausted.

She explained that each person had a piece of paper that we would fold into three sections. Only one section would be visible to whoever was drawing. At the end, we'd unfold it and see the "exquisite corpse" of some creature that we had unknowingly created.

"Now, first everyone draws a head. This can be any kind of head that you like, an animal, an insect, a monster, or a human. Use your imaginations!"

I started drawing a goofy face. It's really the only thing I can draw. I figured if it was cartoonish, I couldn't be criticized if it wasn't any good.

Lotti was effortlessly drawing away. She was probably doing something really difficult, like a horse head or something. Astrid's face was only a few inches from her page. She was concentrating hard, and her turquoise hair hung around her face like a curtain on a stage, making it impossible for anyone to see what she was doing.

Ms. Crick showed us how to fold our papers in a way that hid what we'd just done.

"Now pass this piece of paper to the person on your left."

I passed mine to Lotti and got one from Astrid.

"This time I want you to draw a body. Again, use your imaginations!"

There were snickers from the boys in class; it didn't take a genius to figure out what their "imaginations" were gonna come up with.

Without even realizing it, I started to draw an insect with legs wiggling out from a lumpy body. I covered it in polka dots.

We folded the papers again and passed them to our left. This time we were supposed to draw some kind of legs.

I couldn't think of what to draw, so mine turned into a bunch of octopus tentacles, complete with suction cups.

"Now pass them again, and this time open up the papers and see the wonderful creatures you have created!" Ms. Crick was about to burst with excitement. I don't know what she thought we were going to create here, but there was nothing "exquisite" about what I was looking at.

My cartoonish head was sitting on a bird body with outstretched wings. Lotti had done a really good job making the feathered torso look three-dimensional. The body was propped up on legs that Astrid drew that looked like skinny trees growing up from the ground. There was grass around the trunks where they disappeared into the earth.

The whole room was laughing at their own ridiculous creations. We passed around the other two drawings that we'd made together. Astrid had drawn a head with horns and vines growing out of its eyes. It sat on the insect body that I'd made and had Lotti's long shapely legs in high-heeled shoes. It was hilarious!

The head Lotti had chosen to do was . . . mine. It was perched on a body that Astrid had drawn. It was a bunch of flowers wrapped around a rib cage, sprouting out in different directions; the arms were made of vines and reached out to the edges of the paper. The flowers looked like roses and were really detailed. At the bottom were the octopus tentacles I had drawn. I stared at the picture. It felt real to me, like, more than if Lotti had kept going and drawn my whole body.

"I love this," I said, holding the drawing close to my chest.

"Keep it," said Astrid with a little laugh.

Lotti smiled at me. "It's all yours, Greta."

THIRTY-THREE

Later that night, I had a dream.

I was looking at my family. I realized that I was hovering about twenty feet above them. My parents were laughing as Fej was making all kinds of faces. He was telling a story. I felt myself gently rocking back and forth as I laughed along with them, floating on air that felt strong and slightly solid beneath me. I felt a ripple of calm moving through my weightless body. My mom looked up and smiled at me. She blew me a kiss. Only I could see it. It was like the fluff of a dandelion and when it reached my face it burst open and covered me with tiny feathers. I sneezed and my dad looked up, his eyes squinty and smiley.

"Hey sunshine," he said. "Whatcha doin' up there?"

I rolled into a weightless somersault and drifted down to where they sat around a table covered in a puzzle they were working on. It was a picture of the ocean, nothing but green and bluish-gray waves. I settled effortlessly into one of the lawn chairs and picked up a bright yellow puzzle piece that was shining like a bit of stained glass. I placed it in the middle.

"Perfect!" they shouted. And I woke up.

THIRTY-FOUR

On Sunday my dad had the brilliant idea of taking Fej and me fishing. But not just the normal sit-on-the-bank-of-a-river-holding-a-stick-until-you-die-of-boredom kind of fishing. *No.* We were going to . . . the Trout Rodeo.

Every spring in our town, the city fills up the pond in Meryl Park with tons of trout. There are flyers all over town saying *Come on down to the Trout Rodeo! Enjoy a morning of fishing fun!*

How was this fishing? Don't get me wrong, I'm not a fan of the regular kind. But this seemed like a massacre to me. Hundreds of trout are dumped into the pond, how can you *not* catch one?! But the alternative would have meant going with Mom to pick out curtain rods so . . . yeehaw, I was off to the rodeo.

We stood at the edge of the pond, which was already circled with people holding fishing poles. It reminded me of the game we used to play when we were toddlers. We'd put a pretend fishing pole with a metal "worm" dangling from the end into a bucket full of magnetic fish. Our parents would burst into applause as we brought up a cluster of plastic pieces with googly eyes. "You did it!" they'd say, their smiles beaming, so proud.

This felt basically the same, except with real hooks and blood. It was embarrassing to be there with all these people, staring at my green skin like *I* was the monster, pretending that this was just a harmless game.

"Dad, this is gruesome!" I said.

"It's fine, Greta. We'll just throw them back. It's fun!"

I looked over at a woman standing with her son who was probably about ten years old. They were laughing as the boy yanked a panicked-looking trout out of the pond. It was thrashing its shimmering body at the end of his hook. The mom grabbed it nonchalantly like she was picking an apple off a tree and threw it back in the water. The two of them high-fived.

I suddenly thought of Ms. Binney and *Lord of the Flies*. *Okay*, I thought. *I get it. People are savages.*

Fej started dangling a worm an inch from my nose. "Eat it!" He was laughing. "Mmmm . . . your favorite." He licked his lips.

"Gross!" I yelled, stumbling backward. "Dad!" I whined.

"Jeffrey, that's enough. C'mon, pay attention." My father gently grabbed him by his shoulder and directed his attention to the pond.

In no time, Fej's pole was tugging at his little hands and my dad had to reach over to help him hold on to the rod.

"Looks like you got one, buddy!"

Well, of course he does, I thought. *It's harder not to get one!*

Fej was hooting and hollering like he'd just won the lottery.

They pulled a trout up out of the water and swung it over to where I was standing. It was bouncing and squirming at the end of the line, eyes wild with terror. I saw the flaps of the gills opening and closing, desperate. Water dripped off its silvery body, and the sun was turning the wet scales into a rainbow of colors, like oil in a puddle.

"Okay buddy, take it off the hook," my dad told my brother. But Fej was suddenly squeamish. He refused to touch the fish.

"Ewww!" he said, sticking out his tongue and backing away.

I watched the trout's muscly body vibrating with life under its colorful metallic skin.

I'd never seen anything so dazzling. But its eyes were bulging with fear as its lips pulled uselessly at the air, searching for something it could breathe. I could feel my eyes start to pinch with tears. I couldn't just stand there and watch this creature die.

I reached out and wrapped my green fingers around its slippery skin. I felt its life ripple against my palm and continue, pulsing through the blood in my arm, almost to my elbow.

With my other hand, I twisted the hook out of its mouth, gently, and released it back into the dark, cool water, where it belonged.

THIRTY-FIVE

Lotti, Astrid, and I were eating our lunch in the bathroom. The acoustics in there made it sound like you were holding a microphone every time you talked. Like it was open mic night at the middle school.

"That was so messed up in the cafeteria the other day. You were awesome, Greta," said Astrid. I felt my body stiffen up with pride.

"I mean, what are we supposed to do? It's such a double standard. It's like girls are supposed to just sit and smile no matter what kind of insanity is happening." Astrid made a little fluttery-lashed smile, her hands under her chin.

"Oh my! That's ever so rude, but I'm a delicate flower who never feels anger, because that's *unattractive*, so go right ahead!" We all laughed, and the tiled walls made it sound like we had an audience. Lotti suddenly sat up straighter.

"What if we all go to the dance together? Like a triple date?" she asked, her eyes shining.

"That would be awesome," said Astrid. "I wasn't even going to go, but I'll definitely go with you guys!"

"You won't be upset if you don't go with Evan?" I gave Lotti a knowing look, trying to make it clear that it was okay if she didn't really want to do this. I'd be disappointed, but I would understand.

"I'll see him there," she said, playing it cool. "It's not like we're an official couple . . . yet." She looked at us, smiling and wiggling her eyebrows.

We laughed.

"Perfect!" I said. Forming an alliance in this echoey little room made it feel permanent and official. I pictured the three of us walking into the gym, arm in arm like a wall, just daring anyone to try to test our strength, immune to the scuzzy multi-pawed boys acting like they were in a human petting zoo. We were beautiful and strong as we walked in slow motion like superheroes to the middle of the dance floor. Derek would be plastered against the gym wall, stunned into silence at the sight of my emerald skin glowing against the bodies of my friends, pressed against mine. Everyone would move away, making room for the sheer freakin' glory of the three of us.

THIRTY-SIX

At dinner I didn't even mention that the dance was tomorrow night. I'm sure my parents had gotten a ton of emails reminding them, but it wouldn't have mattered anyway, we were moving soon, and that was all they could talk about. Fej was excited about the new house. I'm sure he pictured himself running and screaming through the "open floor plan" without the inconvenience of having to dodge through things like doors.

I was putting a forkful of noodles in my mouth when my mom suddenly turned to me. "Greta, if that room isn't packed by tomorrow I'm gonna do it myself, and trust me, you do not want that." I sighed and stared at the carrots on my plate that were getting colder and more rubbery by the minute.

"I'll do it tonight," I said.

"Well, I've heard that before," she said, looking to my dad for backup.

He stopped in midchew and gave me a your-mother-has-a-point face.

"No more messin' around, Greta. It's time to get this done," he said.

My whole body went slightly limp as I fought the overwhelming impulse to roll my eyes deep into the back of my head.

"Fine." I sighed.

After dinner, I sat in the middle of my room, surrounded by basically everything I'd ever owned. My mom's fingernails drummed against my door.

"I'm doing it," I said, exasperated, trying to fend off another lecture.

She came in and sat on my cluttered bed.

"Greta. We need to talk."

Ugh. I hated those words. Nothing good has ever come after that phrase. I prepared myself for the worst. She was rubbing her hands together against her chest. Never a good sign. Neither of us spoke for what felt like forever.

She finally said, "I know you've been going through . . . a lot." She reached down, cupping my green chin, stroking it with her thumb. We sat there, looking into each other's eyes.

"It's confusing . . . all of this." She smoothed my curls with her other hand. "I don't understand what's going on with you, Greta. But . . . it's not just your skin that's different, is it?"

I looked into her eyes. And shook my head. *No. It's not.*

I reached up and took her hand that had been stroking my face and held it between my palms, hoping that she'd be able to feel this light, this powerful energy beneath my skin. I smiled at her.

After a few seconds, her brows softened from their worried knot above her eyes and her mouth pulled up gently into a smile. She bit her lip and nodded.

"It's good, Mom. Please believe me."

"Okay," she said.

She let out a long breath. "Well, you better get to work, huh?" She looked around my room.

"Yup," I said.

She got up to go. "'Night, sweetie," she said, looking at me as she closed the door behind her. "I love you."

"'Night, Mom," I said. "Love you, too."

When I scanned the scene around me, I knew there was no way I could get rid of any of this stuff. It would be like tossing a bunch of memories or old photographs into the garbage. I looked over at the pile of empty boxes. Without even thinking about it, I started to pull everything closer to me, forming a nest around my body. I grabbed old shirts and tied the sleeves together. I started twisting the tails of my old dinosaur collection together with a bright pink feather boa that I used to wear for dress up and knotted it with the pant leg of my favorite jeans, which didn't fit anymore. I ripped pages out of my favorite books from when I was little and fanned them around myself. I grabbed an old blanket that my grandmother had made me when I was a baby, that was unraveling from all the years of me absently pulling at the yarn to soothe myself to sleep. I braided the threads through the straps of tank tops and bathing suits. I wove together doll hair and shoelaces. I wedged my stuffed animals between the gaps, forming a wall. It was growing around me like a fort and the more I added, the less I could see of the rest of the room. Before I knew it, it had gotten dark and the only light I could see through a small hole at the top of my cocoon was from the moon, which was full and beamed into my room like a spotlight, cheering me on.

Curled up inside this nest of everything I had, I felt a calm come over my whole body. Like I had been taking short, shallow breaths my whole life without realizing it and was now finally able to breathe deeply. My muscles let go from the slightly clenched state that they were usually in. I felt the small roll of my belly pressing warmly against my thighs. My arms were wound around my soft, hairy shins, and I could feel the sweet warmth of steam drifting down out of my nostrils and landing on my knees. My body was curled into a ball so tight that I lost track of where one part of me left off and another began. My skin was gently pulsing like a heartbeat. Like I was turning inside out.

I twisted and rolled slowly and tightly. It felt so good, so relaxing, and I could feel myself grinning. I felt the pull of long silky wires like veins reaching out from my skin. They touched the random pieces of my room as they brushed up against the sides of my cocoon. *Oh yeah,* I thought. *That's the nose of the doll I got for Christmas when I was four. That's my lucky T-shirt, the one I wore the day Lotti and I became best friends. The day we met.*

All the angles and edges of my body started to melt away, I was softening, getting rounder. My face widened and curved into a soft velvety disc. I was so warm, like my whole body was a blanket, and I fell into a deep sleep wrapped in myself.

I don't know how long I was asleep.

When I woke up, the outer layer of my once-soft body had turned hard, like a shell. I had expanded like foam inside it, taking up every space. I needed to stretch. I pushed and wriggled until I felt it crack, letting in the silvery light from my room. I reached for the edge of the opening, pulling it apart with my legs. I had so many legs! I hoisted myself toward the hole I had made, making it bigger and squeezing out, inch by inch. I could feel the hard edge of the shell scrape against my velvety body as I pulled myself loose. The rim was like the brown lacy edge of a fried egg and once I got my head and arms free, I took a deep breath, like I'd just been born, and turned all my attention to the open window.

I was able to balance perfectly on my six sticky feet holding on to a fuzzy pencil top pointing out from my cocoon. I felt heavy with fluid, and I could feel it moving slightly under my furry skin. Something was slowly peeling off my long, fat body, like the thin membrane from the top of a bowl of pudding left in the fridge. It tugged at my body and unfolded into two small wings, wet and useless against my back. I held on to the pencil, breathing slowly as I felt the fluid move from my thick, liquidy body into the shriveled wings. They stretched and pulled down my back as they grew, and my body got smaller and smaller. My wings started to feel papery as they dried, getting wider and lighter. Out of the corners of my eyes I could see them stretch out on either side of me. They were proud and delicate, edged with a purple line, the same color as the polish Lotti had put on my fingernails days earlier. Finally I felt two long tails, like the ones on a tuxedo jacket, unroll and touch the bottom of the pencil underneath me. My wings were three times the size of my body now. The familiar smell of my room, Tide detergent mixed with the slightly vinegary smell of sweat, filled my tiny lungs. Every cell in my body was focused on the full moon, and the open window.

THIRTY-SEVEN

Un-che, un-che, un-che. The heavy bass of the music inside the gym vibrated through the tiny hairs covering my fuzzy body. From where I was perched on a cool metal shelf under a high window in the school gym, I could see the whole room. I noticed the dorky kid from my bus, Sean Dolittle. He was surrounded by other dorky-looking kids, and whatever they were talking about, they were all *very* into it and didn't even seem to notice that they were at a school dance.

I searched for Lotti.

There were teachers standing in a group near the door, inspecting everyone who came in and out. Their hands were firmly planted on their waists, and they had the serious faces of border police who were *just doin' their job*.

Mr. Lee, the science teacher, was there, but he was completely focused on the food table. His flimsy plate was piled high with pretzels and blocks of cheese, and he was trying to balance a brownie cube at the very top.

I saw Ms. Binney, the English teacher, in one of her beige ensembles, smiling and wiggling her butt back and forth like this club music was her absolute favorite. I'm sure she was just dying to join in but was missing the beloved conch shell that she'd reluctantly left at home. There was an empty space on the dance floor in front of her, like no one wanted to be caught dead anywhere near this woman.

The middle of the floor was a mass of kids jumping up and down in unison to the deep, menacing beat, hands waving in the air. There were orange and yellow streamers and balloons tied to every possible surface in the gym. A desperate attempt to make this sweaty room look like some kind of club. There was a disco ball hanging from the ceiling, spraying colored lights over the crowd.

Because she's so tall, I would have noticed if Sydney Coorly was there. I didn't see her. I imagined that the thought of this many bodies in such a crowded space would be terrifying to her. It would be so easy for one of these boob-obsessed morons to brush up against her, maybe even try to grab at her. I pictured her home, safe. The place where she could finally and completely relax.

I saw Derek, lurking along the edge of the crowd, too cool to be actually dancing. One hand in his pocket, the other one lying heavily on the thin strap of a makeup girl's shoulder.

He kept tossing a wave of hair out of his eyes with a quick jerk of his head. I remembered when that move made my whole body feel warm. The girl kept twisting a strand of hair around her finger and laughing at something he was saying. Having been in what could *barely* be considered a conversation with him before, I can imagine she was giving it all she had to seem interested in whatever he was mumbling. And there was *no way* it was funny.

I remembered the weight of that hand, and it made me stiffen my wings, where my shoulders used to be.

Behind him, on the same side of the room, I could see Evan, in a cluster of boys. He was wearing an actual shirt without a sports team logo in sight. He was talking to one of the boys, but his eyes kept darting over to one particular spot in the dancing hive. It was nothing like Derek's predatory stare. His eyes were soft and smiley.

He was looking at Lotti, who was dancing and laughing with Astrid. She was wearing her favorite sleeveless shirt, which was a shimmering velvet and the red of a Coke can. The long black skirt that she usually wore if she had to dress up was twirling and bouncing around her. She hated fancy clothes and I saw her heavy combat boots moving around underneath the skirt like they were on someone else's body. She was bending and straightening her arms like she was a robot. Her mouth moved like she was making *beep, bop, boop* noises.

Lotti's long dark hair floated around her like a satin scarf, she was freakin' glorious. Astrid had on a black button-up shirt and a bright green tie, her pink hair rolled into two buns up high on either side of her head; her pants were a loud red plaid. The two of them were being complete dorks, not moving to the beat at all. Whatever they were dancing to, it was *not* the song everyone else was dancing to. It was hilarious. People around them would look at each other in a *What's wrong with those two?* way and roll their eyes. I felt my eyes pulse. My love for Lotti made my whole fuzzy body tingle and my wings gently clapped in applause. I watched the two of them flail around, Astrid stomping the gym floor like it was a drum and waving her fingers in front of Lotti's face, making her laugh.

They stopped abruptly, their bodies spontaneously hanging droopy like they had suddenly run out of gas. I could see sweat lining the outside of Lotti's face, making her dark hair even darker.

They nodded and the two of them started heading toward the heavy double doors.

When I flew over to where I knew they would come out of the gym, I saw Derek and the makeup girl. He had obviously convinced her to "get some air" and was standing extremely close to her. His sweaty finger was playing with the strap of her dress. I dove down and started darting around, fluttering furiously in front of his gummy mouth.

He let out a little squeal and swatted at me, but I was too quick. He smacked himself in the face and the makeup girl burst into laughter, genuine this time.

Looking completely embarrassed, he stormed back into the gym just as Lotti and Astrid opened the doors to come out. The makeup girl right behind him, still laughing.

I pulled my wings together and hovered for a second before expertly gliding down toward my friends. I landed softly on a branch directly above them.

They stood in the light outside the gym doors making them look yellow, steam rising from their sweaty bodies.

"Where the heck is Greta?" I heard Lotti say, panting to get her breath. "She wasn't at school today, she's not answering her phone. I thought she'd meet us here. I hope she's okay." Lotti checked her screen again to see if I had texted her back.

"She's probably just late," said Astrid, trying to reassure her. "Don't worry, Greta will be here soon. I have to go to the bathroom, I'll be right back."

When I saw that Lotti was alone, my minty wings shivered slightly as I gathered the strength to go near her. She was trying to text me again. I glided down until I landed perfectly on Lotti's phone.

"Oh wow!" she whispered. "Look at that!" Lotti slowly rotated her phone to get a look at me from all sides. I turned around and stretched my wings open as far as I could, feeling the pull against my back. She put her phone so close to her face that I could feel the moisture from the steam coming off her skin from sweating on the dance floor.

"Oh my god, it's beautiful." She stood perfectly still, holding me in her hand.

"Amazing," she whispered.

The gym door opened, and I heard Astrid.

"Any word from Greta?" she asked.

"No, not yet. I wonder if she, you know, turned a different color." They looked at each other with anxious faces.

"Whoa! Look at that!" Astrid noticed me still balancing lightly on Lotti's phone, I was slowly opening and closing my wings, feeling the night air gently playing with them, like it was trying to coax me into dancing.

"I know! Isn't it beautiful! Can you take a picture?" Astrid got out her phone and slowly moved closer to me.

"Got it," she said. "I can't wait to show Greta."

Later that night I sat on Lotti's windowsill. Her room, like mine, still looked the same as it did when we were little. The walls were purple, the rug was purple, the curtains were covered in purple flowers. This was all because when Lotti was little she told her mom that her favorite color was "puh-puh"

and her mom thought it was the most adorable thing she'd ever heard.

I watched her dancing goofily while she got ready for bed. She kept checking her phone, to see if I had texted back yet.

Where are you?
Did it happen again?
You ok?

When she didn't see any scrolling dots showing that I was about to write back, she dropped her phone on her bed. It dinged and she quickly picked it back up. It must've been Evan because she got a huge smile on her face and lay down to read it.

I watched her typing away, snorting to herself about something he said that, if I had to guess, was not funny and didn't deserve a Lotti snort. But that's okay. She looked so happy. Evan was sweet, even if he did dress like a doofus. I started crawling slowly inside the window, which was open just enough for me to fit through. Balancing was so easy with six legs, and my wings reminded me that if I didn't want to walk, I could always fly. It was late, and the only light in the room was coming from Lotti's phone. It glowed blue against her face, making it look like she was just a head, hovering above her comforter, disconnected from her body, her black hair fanning around her like dark water. When she was finally finished with Evan, she silenced her phone and put it on the table next to her bed. The moonlight lit up her room. I let go of the windowsill and felt my wings open effortlessly as I glided through the air, riding it like a tiny roller coaster toward my best friend, up and down, up and down. The coattails under my wings fluttered like kites behind me. I landed on the pillow next to her and she opened her eyes.

"It's you again." She gasped. We stared at each other. I saw my reflection in her damp eyes. I looked more like myself than I ever had before. My body seemed to be wrapped in a coat of white feathers, with my wings opening around me like a cape . . . like a queen. I was beautiful, and that beauty was all mine. It wasn't about sex; it didn't make me feel like I owed anyone anything. I wasn't afraid. I was free.

My wings were barely moving as we stared at each other.

I heard her inhale quickly as she noticed that the eyes on my wings looked familiar. Their shape and color were as recognizable to her as if she were looking at the face of someone she'd known her whole life.

"Greta?" she whispered. I smelled her familiar breath, like wildflowers, earthy and sweet. I hopped up and landed lightly on the tip of Lotti's nose, touching her skin with my feathery legs.

I squeezed, gently.

"*Bonk*," she whispered.

I let go and turned toward the window, toward the bright silver light of the full moon, feeling it pull me directly where I needed to go.

EPILOGUE

The half-darkened moon looked like a bowl sitting in the sky, waiting for something to be poured into it. It seemed open and hollow, a comfy place to rest. But I had places to go, people to see.

The streetlights were evenly spaced among trees that were all the same height. It was a stretch to call them trees, to tell the truth. They had just been planted and looked more like sticks with little branches reaching up, holding tufts of leaves like frozen cheerleaders holding up pom-poms. *GO!!!!! Soulless!!!*

It was as if someone had put together a movie set of a suburban neighborhood, something they could easily take down when the movie was finished and make into a scene of some other planet, desolate and empty.

I circled four times before I noticed our car, a gray Toyota

Camry with a dent in the rear door where Fej had slammed it with his baseball bat, thinking that it was metal and couldn't be hurt, like Iron Man.

Every light in the house was on and I could see tons of beige walls, empty. They hadn't had time to hang anything yet. They were distracted. It had been a week since I had disappeared, and it was all they could think about.

In the backyard there was a patio made of rocks that were all the same size, with rounded edges. Even *they* were fake. Who buys fake rocks? What could possibly be the point?

My mom had strung lights around the perimeter, and I wondered if she put them up to bring me to her. I've always loved them, not just at Christmas. They make a place feel magical. I landed on a bulb, its warmth radiating up my furry legs. My parents were sitting in the lounge chairs from the old house. The ones Lotti and I had always sat in. I imagined that the scratchy plastic fabric pressing against the back of my mom's neck as she looked up at the sky was somehow a comfort to her. Maybe it felt like a time when everything she knew was still in place.

She and my dad were holding hands, not talking, just staring into the sky.

I circled down toward them, never in a straight line. I never went anywhere in a straight line. My dad saw me first and squeezed my mom's fingers as he said, "Look at that, Maggie. Isn't it beautiful?" I landed on a potted plant that they'd brought from the backyard of our old house. It looked small and out of place, like it was just dropped from the sky. I opened and closed my wings slowly, feeling their attention settle on me.

My mom's eyes were swollen, like she had been crying. Her hand rested on the worn, wooden handle of the chair, and I flew over and landed on her knuckle. She lifted her arm slowly, careful not to scare me away, and brought it up close to her, gently, admiring my powdery green wings with their hazel eyes that looked a lot like hers. My wings could look like a face, tricking a predator into thinking I was something else. Something much bigger and stronger.

I slowly made my way across her fingers, walking my fuzzy legs over her cool, smooth wedding ring toward her pinkie. She lifted it up closer to her face and I wound myself around it, over and over again. I had to make sure she understood: *I'm here. I love you. Everything is going to be okay.*

She curled her pinkie slightly as I circled and circled it until I was dizzy. I heard my mom inhale a jagged breath and whisper, "Paul . . . I think that this is Greta." Tears were slowly rolling down her cheek and catching on her lips that had turned up a bit, into a smile. My father was probably thinking that my mom was just tired. That they had been through so much and now she was losing her mind.

He just said, "Maybe it is," and held her hand tighter. But he watched us, twirling ourselves together on her hand and he noticed the eyes, and how much they looked like mine.

I lifted myself gracefully off my mom's hand and danced in front of them under the lights, dipping and soaring like I was onstage. I thought about the dance recitals I did when I was little. I was always the kid who got the steps just a tiny bit wrong. I waved with my left hand when it was supposed to be my right. I twirled counterclockwise when the other girls were going clockwise. I was never very graceful *before*, but my parents never cared. I remember them telling me after the performance, when we went out for ice cream, *Greta, you always do things your own way, and it's wonderful.*

I had to make sure they knew it was me, their not-so-graceful, goofy daughter, so I went back and forth between them, my big fuzzy body landing on their noses, right between their eyes. It made them cross-eyed when they tried to see me, so they couldn't help but laugh a little. My feathery antennae made me look like one of those Las Vegas showgirls who strut around a stage in sparkly bathing suits, giant feathers stuck to their heads like cartoon birds. Only mine were actually useful. I could smell with my antennae. I smelled my dad's shaving cream mixed with the parmesan cheese that he usually poured over his noodles until they disappeared. They must've just finished dinner. I pressed my soft round head against his skin.

I flew back to my mom's face. She smelled earthy and wild, like she hadn't showered in a few days. I soaked up that smell so it would last until the next time, when I'd dance for them again and show off my pistachio-green wings, long and graceful. I would remind them that I was still there, I was still Greta.

Then I would glide back up into the wide-open sky . . . beautiful and free.

I'll try to make them understand how happy I am, how I've never felt more like myself.

But it will be impossible.

ACKNOWLEDGMENTS

If it wasn't for my amazing agent and friend, Allison Remcheck Pernetti, this book would have never been written. I tend to make sense of things through their absurdity and often dismiss those thoughts as strange and probably *better kept to myself*.

But when I shared the idea for *Greta* with Allison, she didn't think it was crazy at all. Her insight and steady encouragement reminded me that when something feels right and authentic, chances are it'll make sense to other people, too.

So many things have happened over the course of the last couple of years that made this book an absolute inevitability. One of which was reuniting with my first best friend from fifth grade, Christianna Hannum. Although never romantically, she was my first experience of true love. We were inseparable and the long hours on the phone talking about

Greta and Lotti over the past couple of years brought back the exact feeling of going through middle school with her, navigating all the fun and fear, humor, and confusion. She is an astonishingly sensitive and intelligent reader whose help and suggestions were crucial to writing this book.

I'm so grateful to my amazing editor, Joy Peskin, who immediately "got" this story, and whose enthusiasm and extremely insightful edits brought *Greta* to its final version. Working with her has been a dream.

My children, Mayzie and Lilia, although grown, remember the trials and craziness of middle school like it was yesterday, and like most of us, I think, carry it right beneath their skins. They have been an invaluable inspiration to me since they were toddlers. I'm immensely proud to be the mom of two such fascinating, brilliant, and hilarious people.

And finally, to my husband, Paul. His love, humor, and incredibly imaginative and beautiful paintings have inspired me for over thirty years. Without him, none of this would have been possible.

RESOURCES

Dear readers,

Your body is yours to make any and all choices about, including deciding if and/or when you will participate in any sexual activities or allow another person to touch your body. If you have ever experienced any situations in which someone has touched your private body parts in a way that you didn't want or didn't agree to, then you have experienced a sexual assault. It's important to know that sexual assault does not have to involve sex but can include any unwanted touching of your private body parts. This can also include situations in which you felt pressured emotionally or physically to engage in these types of activities, felt like you were forced to go along with those activities, or felt like you didn't know how to get out of those situations. In all of these scenarios, you were no longer allowed to fully make choices about your body. You have the right to say no to *or* change your mind about any activity involving your body at any moment in time, even if you have engaged in that activity with that person before and even if they're someone you're dating.

Sexual assault can happen to anybody. It happens to people of all genders, ages, races, and sexual orientations. It doesn't matter where you live, how much money you have, or what your relationship to the person is. If it does happen to you, or if it did happen to you, it is important to remember that it is *never* your fault, no matter what you were doing or where you were at the time.

You might feel a lot of different emotions—confusion, anger, sadness, guilt, or even just discomfort in your body. These feelings are completely normal after a trauma and won't last forever. It will be important to talk to somebody like a safe adult, a therapist, or a counselor, so that they can help you get the support you need and can help you work through your feelings. Talking to someone can be difficult, but it can be done in whatever way feels the most comfortable for you. This could mean talking in person, calling on the phone, writing a letter, or sending an email. You might start out by saying, "I want to tell you about something that happened to me. It's hard for me to talk about, so if you can just listen while I talk, I would appreciate it."

Sometimes it can feel hard to share what happened with others; you might worry what they will think or how they will react. And unfortunately, sometimes the person you talk to might not respond in a helpful way. If this happens, it's important to remember that their response is not your fault and doesn't mean that everyone in your life will respond the same way. You may need to find someone else to talk to, and it will be important to keep trying until you find someone who can give you the support and help you need. Your friends and family might need time to work through their emotions (a therapist can help them with this, too), but the people who truly care about you will always put you first and will love and support you.

If you are the victim of a sexual assault, or if your friend tells you they have been sexually assaulted, make sure that you tell your safe adult (a parent, family member, or teacher) so that they can support you and can get help. Sometimes help will look like talking to the police, calling 911, or going to the hospital. This can be very scary, but remember that your safety will be their priority, so you should not have to worry about getting in trouble.

—Dr. Alycia Davis, clinical psychologist